MW01115424

ROBERT
FARRELL
SMITH

BOOKCRAFT

SALT LAKE CITY, UTAH

Everything about this story is completely true.
Except for the sentence before this one.

Library of Congress Cataloging-in-Publication Data

Smith, Robert F., 1970–
Captain Matrimony / Robert Farrell Smith.
  p. cm.
  ISBN 1-57345-969-0
  1. High school teachers—Fiction. 2. Blessing and cursing—Fiction.
3. Marriage—Fiction. 4. Utah—Fiction. I. Title.

PS3569.M537928 C3 2001
813'.54—dc21   2001001450

Printed in the United States of America   72082-6822

10 9 8 7 6 5 4 3 2 1

In the past, I've unselfishly dedicated all my work to my wife, Krista. To be honest with you, however, I feel that those dedications didn't earn me as many points as I was hoping for. This could be due to only one of two things. One: the dedications were poorly written. (I think we can all agree that that explanation seems a little far-fetched.) Or two: the woman I married is smart enough to see through the facade. Shoot. Oh well, maybe I'll impress her with sheer volume.

—*For Krista*

IF ONLY YOU'D BELIEVE IN YOURSELF

Her eyes were like gumballs—blue, round, and tucked back behind her slowly blinking lashes. I was searching my mind for the perfect sentence. I said something about clouds and she laughed.

I was getting closer.

I told her that she looked better than Tiffany Thueson had looked at the stake barbecue. Those were the magic words. She smiled, her mouth giving her eyes something to compete with.

"Andy," she said blushing.

I looked at her knees as she swung her legs rhythmically. The summer heat made her look warm and brown. The tree limb swayed under our weight.

"I love you, Maggie Solomon."

"I love you, Andy," she said in return.

I leaned in and gave her the kind of kiss a sixteen-year-old boy gives a seventeen-year-old girl while hiding in a tree on a perfect Sunday afternoon.

I felt the branch move.

I leaned back and looked at her face—she was still smiling. Then as if I had no control over my behavior, I raised my arms above my head and cheered. I made a joke about being larger than life. She seemed to like that.

"I am Captain Invincible," I hollered, holding my arms out as if I could fly.

In my euphoric state I felt above the laws of nature: I was indestructible. I closed my eyes and saw the future. Then as if I had forgotten every lesson that gravity had fought so hard to teach me throughout my life, I placed my hands on the branch and pushed off soaring into the air. I flew for about four seconds before my body slammed into the ground and my head rolled against the stone fence Brother Walton had been working on for years.

I awoke two days later in the Terrance Grandford University hospital. There were nothing but wires and tubes leaning over me as I regained consciousness. A nurse eventually came round and asked me if I was thirsty.

I never saw Maggie again, and by the time I went home two weeks later she and her family had moved. She wrote me once and told me about her new home in Utah and how there was a boy there named Howie who kept asking to walk her home.

I never wrote her back.

CHAPTER ONE

IN THE BEGINNING

The glossy light against the white painted bricks made the hall look even less churchlike than the chapel with its half-carpeted walls. I sat stiffly on a dark wood chair counting ceiling tiles and wondering why I was here.

One hundred and twenty-four.

Brother Kyle Wag came in through the far glass doors and walked straight towards me. He was a round man with a square head and rectangular legs. Many times I had been tempted to reach out and grab his ankles to feel if they were actually as blocky as they looked. Of course common courtesy prevented me from doing any such thing, and yet . . .

"Andy," he acknowledged.

"Brother Wag."

He stopped walking and looked at the dark plaque with the gold lettering that was plastered to the door next to me. The plaque read: Brittledon Ward Bishop's Office.

"Here to see the bishop?" Brother Wag asked, his boxy shoulders locked in a perpetual shrug.

He was a clever man.

"I am," I answered.

"I hope everything is all right," he said kindly.

"Things are fine," I said. "The bishop just wants to go over a few of the members' shortcomings with me."

"Oh dear." His triangle mouth frowned.

"I'm just kidding," I explained.

"Of course," he laughed. "You've always been sort of funny."

Bishop Harding saved me from having to come up with a clever reply by opening his office door and walking out of it with Sister Frent, the Young Women's president. The two of them exchanged comments about the state of youth standards and then shook hands in farewell.

"Hello Andy." The bishop smiled as Sister Frent walked off. "I'm glad you could make it."

"It is a particularly good TV night," I said, trying to make my sacrifice seem greater than it actually was. "But luckily my copy of the *Ensign* was covering up the *TV Guide*."

Kyle Wag shook his head. He then asked Bishop Harding if there would be any problem with him using the library's copy machine to duplicate his family group sheet.

Bishop Harding graciously gave him his blessing, then ushered me into his office. I took the chair to the right of his desk. Judging by the warmth, it was the same seat that Sister Frent had just occupied.

"Candy?" Bishop Harding offered.

I looked at the well-known bowl of hard candy that he always offered folks and passed. Bishop Harding was too fit and trim to be a bishop. He had the build of a scoutmaster or an activities director. His jawline was big enough to make even his huge amount of hair look lacking. And his easy manner made everyone comfortable and grateful for him. He sat down and put his hands behind his head. I could see that the stitching of his shirt under his right arm was beginning to come undone.

"How do you feel about favors?" he asked.

"I'm all for them," I said.

He laughed with his wide eyes. "I've got a doozy."

I hoped that he was still talking about favors.

"Well, if I can help I'd be happy to," I offered.

"I knew you would," he said with a wink. "But before I go any further I need to tell you that I'm not asking this as your bishop."

"Who are you then?"

"Just a friend that thinks you might be able to help." He leaned forward. "How are you doing since the fire?"

"Fine," I answered dishonestly.

The fire he was talking about had taken place just over a month ago—two weeks before the end of the school year and right on my twenty-seventh birthday. It destroyed Parson High where I had been teaching beginning calculus. The entire place was wasted thanks to the clumsy feet of Robert Bogardus. According to my sources it had been the act of Robert trying to impress Michelle Mott by whipping up a "Bogardus Clay Centered Soufflé," in home economics that had started the fire. Robert had just removed what was to be his final exam from the oven and was strutting proudly across the room. Unfortunately, he tripped over Ashley Wambolt's nearly finished throw rug. Thanks to gravity and momentum, he flew into Emily Johnson's simmering potatoes. The spilling potatoes didn't start the fire, but they did give the home economics class guinea pig an extremely warm bath. That in turn caused Scott Hixson to reach out for the large rodent in concern. The guinea pig didn't appreciate the helping hand—in fact, he bit it. Scott

4

went reeling backwards into Dutch Jones who was making French fries in a portable grease vat. The vat spilled, throwing grease all over and into the fire that Tom Spint had going on the large gas stove. The rest—or should I say, the *school*—was history.

I had been teaching my calculus class when I heard the bells go off. We all meandered from the building thinking it was simply another routine fire drill. It wasn't until we stepped outside and could see smoke billowing from the west roof that we realized it was the real thing.

The fire devoured the entire school with great speed. I remember standing behind the front walkway looking around at everyone and realizing that I had just lost my job. I could see students from my class, their expressions looking more dumbfounded than when I had first tried to explain calculus to them. I spotted a girl in a cape and a boy in tights standing next to the pile of ash that had once been the drama portable—they were acting very sad. I couldn't blame them a bit.

Parson High was gone.

When I had finished my mission six years ago, I fully expected to be a journalist or an architect. But the classes for those careers were filled with guys like me who were hoping to gain the kind of education that might make them impressive in the eyes of the opposite sex. I figured I had been whacked with a stroke of genius when I decided to go into teaching. It made perfect sense, seeing how it would surround me with all the girls working towards the same goal.

My choice did encircle me with ample prospects, but they all seemed to think of me as a comrade, while dating and making eyes at the boys who were smart enough to go for other careers. By the time I figured out that my plan wasn't going to work, I was twenty-five and graduated.

I got my job at Parson High not long after I completed school. According to the statistics I was very lucky. Teaching jobs were not easy to come by at the moment. I ended up employed largely because the superintendent was an ex-military friend of my father. So, while most of the class I had graduated with still had not found work, I was taken care of. My contract even included teaching a course during summer school. Unfortunately the fire had destroyed my job security.

"Andy, you still with me?" Bishop Harding waved from behind his desk.

"Sorry," I apologized. "My mind drifts easily."

"Listen," he said. "I know you've got a lot to think about, but I have a brother that lives in Utah."

Somehow that made everything better.

He realized that he needed to expound and went on. "The town he's in is in desperate need of a teacher. And well, you teach."

"Go on," I encouraged.

"I happened to mention the fire, and the fact that you would be perfect. They would pay you money," he added, as if I might not be aware that Utah had moved from the barter system to actual currency.

"Me move to Utah?" I asked. My words were really more so I could hear them out loud than an honest inquiry.

Utah, to most Mormons, is considered to be the geographical heart of our religion. I had had a layover at the airport there once while going to visit my grandparents in Seattle. But to be honest I don't think spending forty-five minutes eating a cinnamon roll and walking around in the Salt Lake City airport really gives a person an accurate view of what life there could be like. From what I had seen, however, the people had looked normal. I remember seeing a woman reprimanding her child for walking too slow and an elderly man trying to figure out how to work a vending machine.

It had seemed quite regular.

"You could take a little time to think about it." Bishop Harding interrupted my thoughts. "Aside from the regular school year of math they would like you to teach a continuing education summer course starting three weeks from now."

"Three weeks?"

"Nineteen days to be exact."

The idea rolled around in my head like a marble spiraling down a funnel. It seemed as if the mere thought completed me. Such an endeavor would be a total and complete change. I had lived in the East for almost my entire life. This was all I knew. Now however, I was jobless—and restless enough to want to try something different. Spending some time in Utah might just make me a better-rounded person. Besides, I had the facts of life to consider. Those facts being that I was jobless in a market that had far too many people with my skills.

"Andy?" Bishop Harding had noticed my lack of attention again. "Are you still with me?"

"Not for long," I said and smiled.

He didn't get it.

CHAPTER TWO

FIVE HUNDRED TWENTY-FIVE THOUSAND SIX HUNDRED MINUTES

I got the job. It was one of the easiest things I had ever procured. I simply phoned the number Bishop Harding had given me and asked a few questions. Satisfied with the answers they gave me, I informed them that I was their man— *them* being Bishop Harding's brother Tat. Tat in turn asked me a nice selection of questions about my qualifications. He came across as a very nice guy. Although I must admit that he seemed overly interested in whether or not I was an Eagle Scout and how I felt about teaching coed classes.

"I've never taught anything besides coed," I had informed him.

"Excellent."

It looked like I was going to be teaching math at Woodruff High. They also wanted me to teach an interpersonal relationship class to a small group of adults at the community college over the summer. And the town council promised it would pay off every one of my student loans at the end of the school year. I couldn't believe it. I had really walked into a good thing. I took a couple of moments to contemplate the wisdom of "nothing good comes easy," but then I pushed those thoughts away, figuring it was simply my time for a bit of good luck.

Whereas obtaining the job was relatively easy, shaking loose my ties in Charlotte proved to be much harder than I had anticipated. My parents, who lived a couple streets over from my apartment, were completely unsupportive of what they saw as a poor career move.

"Utah?" my mother questioned again, her golden hair perfectly matching the jewelry on her wrist.

"Yep." I used the word for the first time.

She sighed. I knew her well enough to know that she was probably as disgusted by my using the word *yep* as by my moving to Utah. My mother and father had always been extremely vocal about the need for us as strong members of the Church to stay in the East and help build up the kingdom here. In fact, they viewed America as consisting of two countries: the refined East and the rouge West. Any time anyone moved to the West my parents felt as if they had been personally betrayed. Now here was their only child pulling up stakes to spend a year in a town small enough to be unknown to them.

"Andrew," my mother reasoned, "we have always taught you that we are needed in this part of the vineyard. What will our ward here do without you?"

"I'm certain they'll cope."

"You're a strength in this ward."

"I'm the physical facilities coordinator. I check the doors to make sure they're locked after everyone leaves."

"Safety is an important issue these days."

"Mom, it's only for a year. Besides this is at the bishop's recommendation."

"What about your father and me?" she asked, trying to guilt trip me. "Don't we get a say in this?"

"I'm sure you'll say plenty." I tried to at least sound respectful. "But I think this might be a good thing for me."

"For me," she repeated sadly. "There is no *I* in *team,* Andy."

"I wasn't trying to spell team."

"And this job," Mom sighed. "Tell me again what it is exactly."

"Math, and a continuing education summer class. They've already faxed me a contract and agreement. If I stick it out for one year my loans are paid in full."

"Money isn't everything."

"I've heard you say just the opposite before."

"Don't nitpick, Andy," she said, pursing her lips. "I can't believe you feel good about this."

"It'll be an adventure."

There was a heavy sigh followed by a short silence.

"What about Lauren?" She was coming at me from another direction. Lauren was the girl I had met and dated since shortly after my graduation.

"Well . . . "

"Andy, she's a diamond in the rough."

My parents needed to record the conversations that we had so they could study them and make sure not to contradict themselves later on. It had only been a short while ago that my mother and father had begged me to date someone besides Lauren. Not because she wasn't a fine, attractive person, but because she wasn't a Mormon. Now, here I was informing my mother that I was moving to a land where Mormon girls were as plentiful as houses, and she was sticking up for the very person she had wanted me to step away from.

"I thought you didn't approve of Lauren."

"What's not to like," Mom said defensively. "She's a beautiful girl with charm and sophistication. Your father and I are quite taken by her."

"Dad offered me money to stop seeing her just four weeks ago."

"He's entitled to change. Besides," she tried to smile as if this were all just some fun conversation between clever friends, "I'm not sure that you're remembering things correctly."

I was about to accuse her of the same thing when my father walked into the room. He had gone out to get his new car detailed, thus leaving my mother and me to work without him on changing my mind.

"Is it safe to come in?" he joked.

I could have predicted he would say just that. He was predictable, tall, and tan. He had dark hair with silver at the temples and nice teeth. I had gotten my height and teeth from him and my eyes and nose from my mom. Neither of them had been generous enough to pass down their personality. I don't know that I could remember a time when I had not seen my dad wearing a dress shirt and tie. He was constantly in uniform. Father-and-son outings had been a painful part of my growing up thanks to his addiction to neckwear. In the mornings, all the fathers and sons would crawl out of their tents looking disheveled, with slept-on hair and rumpled clothes. But not my dad. No, he always had on a clean shirt and tie with pants so pressed you could sharpen a knife on the crease. I told him once that it embarrassed me how he was always wearing a tie, to which he replied, "You never know when you might leave an impression."

There was truth to his words seeing how the other boys in our ward were impressed enough to start calling me "Dressy Boy." It took me six hard-won fights to put an end to that name.

"Have we arrived at a solution?" Dad asked.

My mother looked down as if my father were the local constable and he had just informed her that everyone she had ever cared for had tragically perished.

"Andy, I'm not sure you're making the best move," he said, after a pause.

"I think it will be," I said.

My mom looked at my dad and attempted to roll her eyes in such a way that it would look as if she did not want me to see, while making sure that I actually did. I really needed to move on.

The conversation never got any better, and in the end I convinced my mother and father of precious little besides the fact that I was moving to Utah.

Sadly, there were moments when I actually looked back on my conversation with my parents with gentle fondness—like when I tried to explain my leaving to Lauren. She took the news of me moving with even less enthusiasm than they had. Although, to be quite honest, I feel she threw unkind words at me with great zeal.

"This is all because I won't convert!" she steamed. "You're leaving me because I won't join your church."

"Lauren, I never asked you to convert."

"Well, I know you wanted to ask me." She huffed loudly.

"I did?"

"Hhhhaaaar," she spat in frustration. "I can't believe I've given you all these months of my life."

She had a point. Lauren was the kind of girl that guys invented. She was smart, funny, and great to be around. She made every picture that had ever been taken of the two of us look like it was instantly fit for framing. I had first seen her at the public library right after I graduated. I had gone there to work on my resumé. Ten minutes into my embellishing, I spotted her sitting cross-legged on the floor flipping through books of poetry.

I saw the sign.

I told her poetry read better if you recited it out loud. She took the challenge and read to me well into the night. My resumé had received low marks, but I seemed to have scored well in other ways.

We had dated for a while now and even though I didn't want it to end, I knew it was going nowhere. The main reason for this was the fact that not only were she and her family not Mormon, they were "whisper to everyone else about what weird people Mormons are" kind of folks. In the social slot they occupied, Mormonism didn't fit. They just didn't have me pegged. Despite her family's dislike of my religion, Lauren seemed to care for me. She claimed that she was above the boxes we as humans tend to put each other in, and that her love for me felt no fear from my being Mormon. She had even told me once that the only person she found more attractive than I was the poet Gonzala Heratio. She had then asked, in a rather condescending voice, if I knew who he was. I went with the untruth.

"Of course I know who Gonzala Heratio is," I told her. "Who doesn't?" I had since spent some considerable effort in trying to find out who he was and what he looked like.

"You can't leave, Andy," she pleaded.

"It's only for a year." I tried to soothe her.

"Right," she snapped. "You'll come back with four wives."

"Lauren."

"Andy, I know how many Mormon girls Utah has."

"I'm not going there for the girls."

"Is that what your church teaches you to say?"

For a moment her brown eyes gave me reason enough to rethink what I was doing. I shook it off.

"One year, Lauren."

"I'm not happy," she said.

I wanted to say the same, but strangely I was really looking forward to the adventure that lay ahead. I saw the whole thing as a kind of religious Peace Corps. I would go out west and teach them of the eastern lifestyle while they in turn taught me how to live like a true westerner. It was simply something I needed to do to round off my life.

"I'm sorry." It was the best I could do.

She one-upped me by ripping off the necklace I had given her and hurling it in my direction.

"Don't write me!" was the last thing she said before she stormed off.

I drove to the stationery store and spent over an hour trying to find stationery that didn't look feminine. I think I succeeded.

CHAPTER THREE

THUNDER STRIKES

O nce the threat of family and girlfriend were behind me everything seemed to run pretty smoothly. I said good-bye to the friends I had and gave a final talk in my ward. I think people actually were going to miss me, or at least they did an adequate job of making me feel that way. Bishop Harding promised me the calling of my choice when I returned. I told him to leave the position of ward greeter open.

I moved most of my stuff into a storage shed that my friend had and considered the slate of my life clean and ready to be drawn upon. I hopped into the old car I had had since high school graduation and headed out.

I had prayed long and hard the night before for the heavens to keep my car running all the way to Utah. The car was old and had already given me more trouble than it was worth. In fact the only thing that worked really well was the stereo—that and the rearview mirror, the same mirror I kept looking in as I drove. I watched the past grow smaller and smaller with each mile. Eventually the view became unfamiliar.

The road trip west did a fantastic job of displaying the

entire spectrum of what God's hand could do with a little earth and some time. I left the rolling forested green for the flat open belly of our nation. Then, right as I began to feel that I could stomach flat no longer, the landscape began to break and rise into the desert that most maps and humans call Utah.

It had taken me three full days to get to the border, but only three full minutes to begin to wonder what I had done. Utah wasn't completely brown, but if you pooled all the small pockets and patches of green that it did possess, you would come up with what was still a far cry from the landscape I had left behind.

I passed very few signs of civilization. Not long after I passed a small town called Green River, I realized I just might be lost. I took the next exit and used the excuse of needing to get gas to ask for directions. I filled up my car and wandered into the small shop to pay. Two young boys sat behind the counter playing cards.

"Can we help you?" the short, younger-looking one asked.

I grabbed a bottled water and set it on the counter. "This and the gas."

"That's good water," he said. "Real good. Funny though, who would've thought the day would come when people would have to pay for water? Boy, times sure have changed."

I wondered what times he was referring to, seeing how he could not have been on this earth for much more than sixteen years.

"I was hoping you could help me," I said. "I'm looking for Thunder City."

Any signs of life from behind their eyes completely vanished.

"Thunder City, Utah," I clarified.

"Now I don't think I've heard of . . . Barney, you know where a Thunder City might be?" he asked his friend.

Barney clearly didn't know that plus a lot of other things.

"To be honest with you, son, we just moved to this part," the boy continued.

It was a little disconcerting to have a kid calling me "son."

"We bought the business from the Johnsons," he went on. "Do you know them?"

"Actually no," I answered.

"Big family in this part. Seems you can't toss a rock around here without beaming one of them. Not that I'd want to do such a thing," Barney reassured me. "Sure they might not have given our family as sweet a deal as they claimed," he went on under his breath, "but a done deal is a thing of the past."

He paused just long enough for me to try and steer the conversation back to where it had begun. "So do you know where Thunder City is?"

"Nope. Let me ask May. May!" he called.

Not to sound weird, but an extremely cute elderly woman emerged from the back room and approached the counter. She looked like the kind of person who would at any moment pull out a surprise platter of cookies from behind her back and offer you one. Her eyes winked in her aged face. She had on a plain dress with a rose pinned to the lapel.

"May, this young man here wants to know about a place named Thunder City."

Feeling that a partial explanation was in order I said, "I'm going to be moving there."

"Mishap." She smiled at me.

I couldn't tell if she was commenting on my decision or cursing me.

"*Mishap* is the nickname of Thunder City," she explained slowly. "You go west about twenty miles and turn left on the 27." May pointed with a wrinkled finger. "You'll take that for about forty miles and then run smack-dab into it."

"So Mishap *is* Thunder City?" I asked, seeking clarification.

She smiled again. Then with all the wisdom her age afforded her she sensed the need to go into greater detail.

An hour later I was on my way to a place affectionately called "Mishap." I was feeling slightly jilted by the fact that the town I had been anticipating had such an unflattering nickname. To be honest, I wouldn't have minded if the new name were more like, "Hidden Sunset" or "Paradise Found," but "Mishap"?

I began to search the clear sky carefully as I drove. I felt confident that if I were to look closely enough I might be able to actually catch heaven laughing.

I decided to keep my eyes on the road.

CHAPTER FOUR

MISHAP, UTAH

N ot long before he died, Brigham Young sent a thickheaded farmer named Cornelious Thunder out to the Pinched Basin region in Utah to establish a town.

Cornelious did just that.

He picked a spot between two high red cliffs and at the bottom of the basin. Then when no one was around he lifted his arms to the heavens and asked God, "Does this have to be the place?" His answer came in the form of two black crows flying headfirst into one another. Cornelious felt this was unusual enough to qualify as a sign. He also was just stubborn enough to make the new town work. He stuck to his guns and with hard work and sheer determination created what became known as Thunder City, Utah. For many years Thunder City flourished. The red cliffs kept the wind out and the soil together. Trees grew fast and soon what was a shabby piece of desert turned into a spotty green haven people couldn't help but whistle at.

Wearing the blinders of everyday routine, few folks stopped

to realize that the entire population of Thunder City was Mormon. This fact became glaringly clear when only a few years back a German immigrant named Reinhold Hap wandered into town looking for a piece of good land to settle on. He had discovered Thunder City one night while surfing the Net in Munich, Germany. The city's home page (yes, it had a home page!) made this piece of Utah look like the perfect all-American town. It also promised low cost property. Reinhold arrived and bought one of the nicest plots in town, plus a pair of cowboy boots and a matching hat. He built his dream home on his land, which was located near the public library and two blocks over from the city park.

Well, as time rolled on people began to notice and grow curious as to why Reinhold didn't attend church. The bishop actually put sacrament meeting on hold while he sent out the elders quorum to see what was up. When they reached his house Reinhold answered the door and informed them of three things. One and two were that he wasn't a member of their church, and that he would have told them so if only they had asked. Three was that they were interrupting the rerun of *Night Rider* that he was watching. The elders quorum, for the first time in as long as anyone could remember, was silent.

Few knew that there were those in their midst who watched reruns of commercial television on Sunday. Also, it had never occurred to any of them that there would someday be a genuine nonmember living in their town. They were thrilled. Finally they had someone to direct their missionary efforts towards. Reinhold Hap was befriended and prodded by everyone in the area. He was invited to all the Church functions. He was also the guest of honor at Celebrate Reinhold Day. Committees were formed and prayers were offered in pushy earnest, and all on behalf of Reinhold and his unconverted soul. The ward even had a barn raising at his house despite the fact that he already had a barn and didn't need another. In the eyes of Thunder City, Reinhold was an honorary "brother," on his way to becoming the real thing.

Reinhold took it all in stride.

When he said he wasn't interested, folks would just smile and say things about there being a time and a place when he would be. If he argued that he was happy with his own religion, folks would wink and comment about him eventually seeing the light. And when he wanted to start dating some of the older single Latter-day Saint women in town, folks threatened to ride him out on a rusty rail. They further vowed that the day his gentile hands touched one of their fair women they would stone him, tar him, or drag him down across the border depending on the mood of the mob. It was one thing to have a nonmember amongst you, but it was an entirely different issue if that nonmember had aspirations of fiddling with your women.

A lesser man might have left Thunder City altogether, but Reinhold Hap liked his piece of earth and felt that he was entitled to stay there and pursue his own happiness. So with a couple of well-written letters he struck up a friendship with a woman he had known back in Munich. Impressed by the way he manipulated ink and attracted to the prospect of a home and two barns, this woman traveled across the world and into the arms of Reinhold Hap. They married in the bigger of the two barns with the help of a preacher from three towns over.

With Reinhold married off, the townsfolk figured they could treat him neighborly again. Reinhold wouldn't have it. He insisted that everyone leave him and his wife alone. He also threatened that if he ever caught a single person calling him "Brother" he wouldn't be able to control himself. So in a town full of Brothers and Sisters, there was only one Mr. and Mrs. Hap.

Shortly into the new marriage, tragedy struck the Haps. On a particularly cloudy morning Harriet Hap turned up missing. The back door of their house was torn off and unknown foot-prints were spotted in the wet garden soil. Reinhold swore he had no idea what had happened to her or where she could be, but that didn't hide the fact that she was gone.

The town suspected foul play.

Stones were turned and bushes trimmed in an effort to search thoroughly. After two months of nothing the town put the pins on Reinhold. Surely, he had to know what had hap-pened. Or maybe *he* was the *what*. Everyone knew that things had not been ideal for Reinhold and Harriet. There had been many signs that the marriage was having problems shortly before her disappearance. Those signs now seemed to suggest that something truly bad had happened and that Reinhold was the cause.

There was a short trial that ended in a mistrial and mistrust. Reinhold withdrew, hiding himself up in his house and coming out only to yell at the kids who were brave enough to cross his lawn to buy milk and cheese at the corner store. He claimed Thunder City had ruined his marriage and his life. He cursed everyone, threatening that his misery would be heaped upon the heads of any townsperson who married. He promised nothing but doom and misfortune to those who chose matrimony.

Larry and Tillie Cutler were the first couple to thumb their noses at Reinhold and his curse. They had married in the Salt Lake Temple and had an elaborate reception in Thunder City. After the reception, the happy couple packed into the small plane Larry owned and flew off for their honeymoon and into what should have been a happy future. And it may well have been just that, if not for the small fact that the two of them were never seen again. Their plane simply disappeared and no part of it had yet been found. Exhaustive searches and studies were made; lakes were dragged and theories tossed about like extra pennies into a watery well. There were those who figured the plane had gone down in some small unknown spot within the thousands of miles that the flight plan covered. But the majority of the town figured Larry and Tillie had simply been taken up in the curse of Reinhold Hap.

Everyone was stunned. Reinhold withdrew even further from the community, locking himself up in his big house and showing his face so seldom that few folks remembered what he looked like. The rest of the town mourned, feeling that somehow they were all to blame. It had never been their intention for things to end this way, but when they really looked at it most people seemed to realize just how much their actions had contributed to the end.

The town was bruised.

People might have gone on and on forever, rehashing and recalling the things they had done to make this happen if it hadn't of been for the reappearance of Mrs. Hap.

Of course it wasn't like Harriet to simply walk back into town one day and ask if anyone had missed her. No, apparently she had more flair than that. She first appeared on a stormy night, the apparition of her face spreading across the choppy water of Knock Pond. The image looked like no more than distorted light until one of the youth climbed up on top of Lop Rock and saw to his horror that the picture before him was that of Harriet Hap. The movement of water seemed to contort her face and give her lips shape.

"Marriage," she seemed to whisper. "Marriage."

After she had spoken her piece she faded back into the dark water. But not from memory. Since that night she had appeared many times, always forming across the surface of the pond like some two-dimensional demon. And always whispering the union that had been the death of her.

The townsfolk of Thunder City had attempted to figure out how she appeared and why, but no reasonable answers had ever come of it. But the town talked and thought of her so often that eventually most folks began calling the place "Mrs. Hap."

"Mrs. Hap" became "Mishap" and the city became forever changed—it simply lost some of its thunder.

It was quite a story.

I contemplated just how much of it I should believe as I drove closer to the town that the tale was attached to. The road rose up sharply and then seemed to drop at an interesting incline down into a green valley surrounded by red cliffs. If what I had been told was correct, I had just entered Mishap. I drove down six or seven switchbacks and past a large gully thick with water. Bits of houses began to show through the trees. They looked like frightened children who were hiding as a stranger drove into town.

Despite the fact that everything was so completely different from what I had left behind me, I liked it. The red cliffs were as magnificent as any lush green I had ever seen back home, and the trees and grass that did grow seemed so much more impressive considering that they had to fight to be there. The buildings and streets were clean and quaint. I spotted a few businesses that one might spot in any town across the country, as well as some that were most likely exclusive to the area.

As I came to the center of town I noticed a small convenience store called "U-Tote-Em" and pulled in. Now that I was actually here I needed a few more directions. The store was in a brick building with wide front windows and narrow parking slots. I took the farthest space on the left. I got out, stretched, stared at the amazingly blue sky, and walked in. There was a male clerk about my age sitting behind the counter talking on the phone. I appeared to be the only customer at the moment.

"Someone just came in," I heard the clerk say to the person he was talking to on the phone.

Not wanting to interrupt his conversation I simply waved and gave a small nod as I walked past the counter and down the candy aisle.

"He just waved at me," he informed whomever he was talking to.

I looked at him out of the corner of my eye and shrugged. I then stepped to the glass refrigerator and opened the door.

"He's getting a drink," the clerk reported. Then after a pause, "I don't know. I can't see."

I made my choice and turned towards him.

"Root beer," he whispered. "Could be. No, no. He's coming closer. Closer . . . he stopped at the candy bars."

I stopped and looked around feeling incredibly self-conscious about this clerk and his keeping track of me.

"I think he's going to get a candy . . . no, he's coming closer. He's almost . . . gotta go." He hung up the phone and smiled at me.

I awkwardly set my stuff on the counter.

"How's it going?" he asked me.

"Fine, I guess."

"You're like me," he said, looking at my drink and punching some numbers into his register. "I guess a lot. There's just no way for us to know everything."

"Good point." I smiled. "I'm Andy Phillips," I said, sticking out my hand.

"Gordon," he said, doing the same.

The name fit him perfectly. He could never have been a Rick or a Jared, he was just too Gordonish. His hair had slid back exposing more forehead than face, and from the looks of it the recession wasn't over. He had lumpy ears and a nose that competed with his mouth to be the largest feature on his face. He looked to be about twenty-eight, which would make him my senior by almost a year. His apron appeared almost as worn as his expression.

"Do you know where the Harding house is?" I asked.

"Sure," Gordon said. "If you turn around and look out those windows you'll be staring right at it."

I turned and stared.

"Well, I guess I don't need you to draw me a map then," I joked. I turned back and he stared. For the second time in the same day I felt compelled to explain myself. "I'm going to be staying there."

"You talk as if you might not be from around here," Gordon said. "I mean you've got an accent or something."

"I'm from Charlotte."

"Don't know her," Gordon said.

"Actually it's not a her, it's a place. Charlotte, North Carolina."

"Oh that Charlotte," he recovered.

I decided I liked Gordon.

"Is this your store?" I asked as I looked around.

"It is," he replied proudly, waving his arms so as to display his kingdom. "Of course it's not really mine yet. I'm paying the bank and all. I'll be making ten years of set payments plus a certain percent of the net sales. *Net* means . . . well, I'm sure you know what *net* means."

"I think I do," I said for his sake.

"Whew."

I glanced around at what was there. Aside from the unusually huge selection of circus peanuts, I could have been standing in almost any convenience store in America. I spotted a paint-striping truck outside the store. It was a large, white vehicle with an extended arm that looked as if it were spraying lines on the road. It came our direction slowly, painting the asphalt with precision. Right before it passed the store, it swerved, pulling into the parking lot and stopping right next to my car. It was so close to my vehicle that for a moment I thought it had hit it. A burly looking man, with a face so full of hair that it looked like he was wearing a mask, got out of the truck and came into the store.

"Howdy, Gordon," he hollered.

"Hey, Wilson," Gordon said. He then turned to me and said, "That's Wilson."

"Oh." I would have introduced myself, but Wilson was now on the other side of the store picking up a display of chips he had knocked over.

"Wilson Phelps," Gordon elaborated.

I was about to add something else to the conversation when I spotted an older man in a postal uniform coming across the street on foot. He waved at a car that nearly hit him and then walked up to the parked paint truck and stared at the back of my car. He hurried inside.

"Gordon, who's driving the stripper today?" he asked with concern.

"Wilson," Gordon pointed.

I saw Wilson over by the fountain drinks trying to go unnoticed.

"You forgot to turn off the paint again," the postman chided. "We've got a double yellow coming right up to the store. Remember what happened on Elm street?"

"It faded eventually," Wilson said sheepishly.

I finished paying as the postman went over some very common rules of mastering the art of striping streets. As I made my way to leave he took hold of my elbow and acknowledged me.

"I hate to sound nosey, but I was just on the phone with Gordon and we were wondering if you might be the new teacher?"

"I am."

"Well, that's great," he said excitedly. "I must admit you're much taller than I thought you would be. Plus I pictured you with glasses."

"My eyesight is weakening," I joked.

He seemed happy that I had said that.

"I'm Tat Harding. My wife Phyllis and I have the home across the street where you'll be staying." He pointed in a completely different direction than Gordon had. "I believe you and I spoke on the phone a couple of weeks ago."

"How's my brother doing?" he asked.

"Great."

Tat shook my hand and patted me on the back, allowing us

both time to look each other over. He didn't look at all like Bishop Harding's brother.

What I saw was the quintessential, stereotypical, all-American, older-than-middle-age-looking mailman. He had long, bushy sideburns that brushed up against the grin he wore comfortably. His uniform was pressed and clean, the shine on his shoes dimmed only under the light of his eyes. He had even put on a tie that clearly was not intended to go with the actual getup—it clashed terribly. He stood on small feet, but waved rather large hands as he spoke.

What he saw was a brown-haired, blue-eyed, six-foot-and-two-quarters-of-an-inch easterner that was wondering what he was doing out west.

"It's nice to finally meet you, Tat," I said honestly. "So is Tat short for something?" I asked.

"Nope. Just Tat. Tat Harding. It's spelled the same front ways or back. That's the Tat part," he clarified. "Harding backwards would spell *Gnidrah*. And I don't think that's a word. Of course I don't know any other language besides English. It could be an Asian word of some kind. What am I saying?" he slapped his forehead. "You're the teacher. You would know. Is it Asian?"

"I don't think so," I smiled.

"You and me both," he patted me again. "I like you, Andy. I knew you would be perfect for our town the moment I first heard your funny talk. We've been needing you."

"Well I'm excited to do my time."

"I like that," Tat grinned. "I bet they teach you teachers all kinds of clever ways to say simple things. 'I'm excited to do my time.' That's great. Well, we're here for you."

"I appreciate that," I said honestly. "In fact I was wondering if someone could sort of fill me in on the summer term I'll be teaching." I paused to make sure he was up to speed. "I know you wanted me to start Monday. You had talked about faxing me some papers covering what I would be teaching and to whom. But I never received anything besides the contract for the full year term."

"Don't worry about all those, 'what ifs,'" Tat said. "The council has got it all figured out."

"The council?"

"The Council of Seven," Tat said solemnly. "But that's not important at the moment. The important thing is that you'll have no problem. None whatsoever. Just rest easy knowing that you're in good hands."

I looked over at Gordon who was cleaning his fingernails with the can opener that was tied to the register with a string. Just beyond him was Wilson who was desperately trying to stop the fountain drink ice dispenser from running over. Finally I looked at Tat as he smiled and winked.

I would be lying if I didn't admit that I was a little nervous about the hands I was in. I smiled so as to reassure them that I was all right with all this, falling back on my lifelong habit of making others comfortable at my expense. I would have held the smile longer than I did, but a car speeding down the street demanded my attention. I watched it roll along the road following the mispainted yellow line. It swerved with the curve and plowed right into the back of the paint truck. With a metallic thud it pushed the truck—all the way through the front window of the store. Glass cascaded down like screaming rain. Before any of us could properly gasp, a second car made the same mistake and plowed right into the first car. The casualties were greater with this blow as it pushed the truck deeper into the store. The large display of two-liter soda pop bottles were crushed under the front fender of the paint truck. Soda bottles burst and exploded like sticky fireworks. I saw a pop cap clip Tat right on the forehead just before I got drenched with what smelled like orange syrup.

Tat raced out of the building, hoping to prevent anyone else from making the same mistake as the first two cars. Gordon began hollering at Wilson Phelps for his poor paint job, while those involved in the wreck climbed out of their vehicles and began discussing whose fault was whose. I slipped out and looked over at my car that was now pinned in by the pile up. A third car ignored Tat's waving arms, and again the sound of crumpled metal and glass sounded out.

Since no one was seriously hurt, and because I didn't want to get too involved too fast, I worked my way through the wreck and pulled my suitcase out of the back of my car. I threw my backpack over my shoulder and headed across the street to the Harding house.

If pressed, I would have to admit that I had made quite an entrance.

If pressed, mind you.

CHAPTER FIVE

HOME SWEET HMMM . . .

When Cornelious Thunder was first faced with the task of naming Thunder City, he choked. He was fine with the plow and horse and not half bad at building homes and furniture. But in the creativity department Cornelious had a real problem. So, at the prompting of his wife, he took a couple of weeks to just look around and wait for something inspiring to strike him. Surely, God would help him with a name.

Cornelious observed the tall red cliffs, as wide, unbridled sunsets bled into them. Nothing. He spent a full afternoon walking the banks of the Wayne River. He studied the pools of clear water that lay like silver coins against green velvet. He was coming up empty. He stood for hours in the fields watching the calming winds blow celestial patterns over the growing vegetation. Nada. In frustration, Cornelious spent a few hours in the closest town a number of miles to the west. He received no inspiration in the actual town, but he felt that it was fate tickling him on the feet when, on his way out, he passed the town sign that said quite plainly, "Dortonville: Gateway to the West."

32

Cornelious was thrilled. He raced home to publicly declare to all who would listen that their home now had a name.

"Cornville: Gateway to the East."

People clapped and cheered. A few even got teary. But in the morning when heads were clearer and maps were brought out it was made apparent to Cornelious that their town wasn't actually a gateway to the East. At very best it was an alternative route to the southwest. Cornelious was crushed, not so much by what they were saying, but by the fact that now he had to think of something else. Luckily for everyone, his wife suggested he just go with his last name. And with that Thunder City was born.

The Harding house was a wonderful thing simply to look at. I had seen pictures of large Victorian homes before, but not a single one of those pictures came close to portraying the amazing structure that now stood before me. It was four stories, not including what looked to be a basement or the small space that rose up above the top of the roof. Trees as tall and as complicated as the structure they shaded rustled their leafy hands in the light wind, looking like attendants who were consumed with caring for the great house. I watched a bird return to a thick nest that was stuck up under a third floor overhang. It sang a moment, seeming to brag about what a posh spot it had happened to find.

I stepped up onto the large wraparound porch and read the four gold plaques that were glued near the left door frame.

1717 Angus Road
Post Office
Boarders welcome
Step inside

I stepped through the front doors as if making a personal leap into someplace that I knew would do me good but would still cause me pain. The foyer was lined with post office boxes and posters advertising different stamps you could purchase. There was a long wooden counter with an open window in the middle of it. I walked up to the window and rang the small bell that sat there. It made a hollow thud. I was about to pick up the bell to see if I could make it perform better when a large feminine head appeared in the window. I tried not to look too startled. The woman had an extremely full head of gray hair. It was all pulled up and twisted into what I assume was some sort of style. I counted at least seven pencils pushed into her hair at different points. She had the freckled nose of a twelve-year-old surrounded by the face of a woman in her late forties. I could tell that smiling came easy to her because she tossed out a half dozen before I even got a single word in.

"Hi, I'm Andy Phillips. I'm looking for Phyllis."

"Guilty," she confessed. "Please, call me 'Phil.'"

Phyllis stuck her right hand out to shake mine. Three of her fingers were topped with rubber thimbles and there were at least fifty rubber bands around her wrist. She was obviously hard at work.

"It's nice to meet you," I said. "I wrote you about a room."

"You sure did. Tat and I have been anxiously awaiting your arrival," Phyllis said, setting down the stack of mail she had been holding in her left hand. "Let me just find my keys."

She disappeared from view only to emerge a few seconds later from behind a dark oak door next to the packing supplies display. She motioned for me to come with her up the stairs. I picked up my suitcase and followed.

"We're excited to have you staying here," she said kindly as we hiked. "The whole town has been abuzz about you coming to straighten things out."

Her wording made me uneasy. But I was too busy listening for signs of Phyllis becoming out of breath to worry about it immediately. She kept an even breath and continued talking.

"Yep, we're feeling pretty pink knowing that we've got you. You're a feather in our cap. We'll show fate that we're not just going to sit around doing nothing."

"I'm excited to be here." It was all I could think to say, not fully understanding what she was talking about.

We turned another corner, climbed some more stairs, and then stopped in front of a white door. It took Phyllis a couple of tries to find the right key on her ring.

"I hope this room will work for you."

"I'm sure it will be fine."

"This used to be our daughter Summer's room," Phyllis said suddenly sober. "She's gone now, you know?"

"I'm very sorry to hear that." I tried to comfort her.

"Thanks, Andy," she sighed. "But it'll be okay. She just lives down the street. Sarah, our other daughter, stays in the basement bedroom with our one and only grandchild, Markus. Cutest kid you'll ever lay eyes on. In case you're curious, however, there's no father figure around any longer. He turned out to be a real dud. Of course you may already have figured out that marriage has a hard time taking root here. Poor Sarah,"

Phyllis tisked. "She's always been a little thick in the head, bless her heart. We love her so."

"That's kind of you," I lightly joked.

Phyllis turned and looked at me. "I like you, Andy. Tat's been talking to everyone about how inspired it is to have you here. I'm feeling like he might actually be right."

She finally found the key and stuck it in the lock. With one turn and a small, "Violà," the door flew open. I think I liked it better closed. The room was completely pink. Stuffed animals littered the floors, shelves, and windowsills. A pretty white desk with a purple vanity sat in the corner overshadowed by the frilly canopy bed with heart printed drapes.

I tried not to look disappointed. I had been told that my room and board would be free, but at the moment it looked as if it were going to cost me my dignity.

"I'll change the sheets and empty the wastebasket once a week. Everything beyond that is your responsibility," she explained. "The bathroom is down the hall, and we have a family dinner every night at seven sharp. I know it's a bit late, but food sits better with Tat when he eats after seven. You're always invited. In fact, we might feel real bad if you don't show up."

I would have said something, but I was still thinking of a nice way to say that this room just wouldn't work. Phyllis took the key off the ring and handed it to me.

"If you lose this key just ask around," she said. "There are a lot of people walking around town with a key to this room. After Summer went off to school we started renting out the place. Most folks never returned their keys. I think the extra jingle in their pocket makes them feel important."

She shook her large key ring in my face and smiled. Then as

if she sensed that I needed to be alone with my new feminine side she brushed past me and started down the hall.

"Let me know if you need anything," she offered as she retreated.

I managed a "Thank you, Phil."

"Phyllis," she corrected.

"Thank you, Phyllis. You may not want to count on me for dinner tonight. It's been a really long couple of days."

"Suit yourself, but you'll want to watch for a warm plate of leftovers that someone just might leave by your door."

"I'll be on a constant vigil."

I walked into my room and set my suitcase on the desk, hiding the large purple vanity. It wasn't much, but surprisingly it seemed to help.

CHAPTER SIX

WELL, AT LEAST WE'RE GATHERED

The first church house in Thunder City had been a log cabin that Cornelious Thunder had originally built for his mother-in-law. She refused to live in it due to the leaning walls, and so Cornelious graciously donated it to the Church. When the number of members grew too large for the cabin to accommodate them, the town built a chapel made from river rock on the banks of the Wayne River. The Utah sky as a backdrop made every stone look important. Unfortunately the construction of the building was not really of the highest quality. During a ward activity, Sally Weston's crazy mare broke loose from the corral and ran towards the scent of water. Deciding that a straight line was the shortest path between here and there, the animal ran right through the building. With an accidental breezeway now running through the middle of the chapel, the remainder of the rocks acted in a very Christian manner and leaned on each other. Off balance and structurally lacking, the entire church house crumbled into the Wayne River. The chapel ruined what had once been the prettiest spot along the banks, but it created a large alcove for better swimming. Two years later Jonathan Skew completed the chapel that still stands today.

I hate to admit it, but I don't remember ever having such a nice night's sleep. Of course waking up was a bit confusing. It took me a moment to remember that the pink frilly room was not some sort of dream gone wrong. I had to move my suitcase and look in the mirror to make sure I wasn't a ten-year-old girl with braids and braces.

I shuffled to the window and looked out on my surroundings. The town looked empty and thin. Just as I began to think that I could simply will it all away, the sun appeared, rising like the bald head of a curious neighbor. Its light seeped slowly into every crack and line the night had created. Colors that I had not seen before seemed to seep up from the earth, bleeding into the new sky.

I watched a young boy pedaling his bike toward the house. He was loaded down with a satchel full of Sunday morning newspapers. He flung one in the direction of the Harding house. I considered sighing contentedly over what a picture-perfect small town this was, but just then the paper boy hit a rut and flew forward off his bike. I watched him pick himself up, collect the scattered newspapers, and ride off into the distance.

I put on my wrinkled suit and then closed my eyes to decide between the two ties I had brought. I was pleasantly surprised with the choice I finally made. I finished dressing and worked my way downstairs. I only got lost twice.

Tat was at the bottom of the stairs complaining about Phyllis making him wear a belt to church.

"These pants aren't going to fall down."

He had a point. I think the one thing a person wearing dress pants with an elastic waistband doesn't need to worry about is having them accidentally fall down.

"So, what time does church start?" I asked.

"Our ward begins in about fifteen minutes. So, if you start walking now you'll be no more than a couple of minutes early. It's about three blocks east down by the drugstore." Tat fastened his belt and looked at himself in the long mirror near the front door. "This looks just plain silly. There has got to be a better way."

I left him to fight with fashion on his own—I stepped outside and welcomed the day like a debutante bowing to her first dance. I was honored simply to be here. I walked past Gordon's store and noticed that he had already replaced half the broken windows. My car still sat there empty and quiet. I decided to just leave it there for a while. It seemed like a good challenge to see how long I could live without transportation in a small town.

As I walked to church I observed people strolling and slowly driving down the well-manicured roads. All of us were heading off to worship the very being that had given us the will to get up and go.

When I came around the bend and saw the church for the first time I actually gasped. I would love to say that my reaction was brought on by the fact that angels were pacing the rooftop or that I had caught the entire building being translated and lifted up. But no, my gasp was born of reasons far less heavenly. There is just no subtle way to say it. The Mishap chapel was a bigger architectural monstrosity than I had yet encountered in my life. It looked like a huge overturned boat with a thick, twisted spire on the west end. The spire was doing the most undignified job of pointing towards heaven that I had ever seen. It pointed as if blaming the fates for placing it there. There were small round windows running along the entire side of the building. Around each window was what appeared to be a pirate ship's wheel. The whole thing looked like a nautical museum gone terribly wrong. I glanced around wondering if this was all some elaborate joke that the entire state of Utah was pulling on me.

Sadly, that didn't seem to be the case.

In the short time I paused to catch my breath Tat and Phyllis had caught up to me.

"Sort of makes you wonder," Tat said wistfully.

"About what?" I asked, as we stared at the chapel.

"About what it would be like to live a life on the sea."

"Is that the purpose of chapels?" I joked.

Tat ignored me. "It was built by a man named Jonathan Skew. He was a famous shipbuilder back in the early part of the century."

"What was he doing here?" I asked, seeing how we were a good distance from any actual seas.

"He retired here. This was the last thing he ever built."

I figure heaven must have struck him dead after viewing his work.

"It's built just like an upside-down boat," Tat explained.

"I can see that."

"Nothing gets past you, Andy," Phyllis said. Her gray hair was pulled up and twisted into a peak with a fuzzy clip. She had on a purple dress made of material that looked like it would be perfectly suited for making beanbags. I looked at Tat and realized that he had a burnt orange sash pulled through his belt loops and tied at the waist.

"I see you found a substitute for your belt," I said.

"Tat doesn't stop until he's solved the problem," Phyllis complemented him. They leaned in and kissed one another. I took that as my cue to continue on my way. I stepped up the walk and through the double doors. The official name of the Church was spelled out on the foyer wall with what looked to be rope. Below the name two short couches sat stiff and boxy. One couch held a woman with a purse bigger than her lap, the other a pile of hymnbooks and a fanned-out spread of programs. I took one of each—a hymnbook and a program that is—and walked into the chapel. You'd think that I would have become so used to gasping that I wouldn't have been surprised to hear myself do it again.

That wasn't the case.

It was a nice chapel, with big organ pipes up above the front and a nice-looking pulpit that was considerably higher than most I had seen. What had startled me was that all the backs of the pews were at least five feet high. From where I stood I couldn't see a single person, just rows and rows of dark high-backed benches. The pews gave the tall pulpit purpose, seeing how there is no way anyone could have seen someone speaking from a normal one. Finding a seat was rather embarrassing because I had to walk to the end of each row to see if they were actually empty or not. Everyone stared at me as if I was intruding on his or her personal space simply by looking. I finally found an empty spot on the side near the front. Once seated I couldn't see anyone else besides the people in the rows directly across the aisle to my left. I should add that I don't think they were pleased by my presence. From the looks of it, they were used to having more privacy than I was now affording them. They appeared to be finishing off bowls of breakfast cereal. They glared at me. I was so bothered by the situation that I considered getting up and walking out.

While contemplating my escape, however, a short man in an extremely light suit climbed up to the podium and welcomed us all there. From the vantage point of the podium I felt confident that this brother had an extremely clear view of the tops of everyone's heads. I ran my fingers through my hair hoping to make a good first impression.

"Welcome to Thunder City First Ward," he said cheerfully. "We are happy to have you all in attendance.

I looked at the few "you alls" I could actually see. They had all finished their breakfast and were looking reverently at the speaker. This made me feel a bit better.

"I'm Bishop Hearth," he said. "With me on the stand is Brother Crammer, my first counselor. Brother Farrelly is out of town selling off a bit of his livestock. We wish him luck with his goats."

Despite the fact that I couldn't really see anyone, the place had a nice feel to it. We sang an opening hymn and partook of the sacrament without any disruptions. I was pleased to see the large number of deacons in the ward. The one passing the sacrament to me, however, gave me a start due to the fact that he had not yet reached the height of accountability. I didn't see him until he suddenly popped into the pew.

After the sacrament, a Sister Moore approached the pulpit and began giving us an earful in regards to repentance and what it had and had not done for her. I took some time during her talk to really study the bench I was sitting on. The high back was intricately carved and polished. The wooden picture was that of a fisherman in a boat throwing out a net. I would have thought that it was supposed to be a depiction of the Savior, but the person in the carving was wearing overalls and holding a lunch pail.

Thanks to the benches, I found myself feeling incredibly cut off from the congregation that I had been hoping to bond with. Having no one to look at and check up on in front of me, and having the freedom of no prying eyes from behind, I found myself sitting in a far more relaxed position than I normally would have. If I pushed my body over a bit I was almost completely hidden from the members that were across the aisle. I rationalized my behavior by blaming it on the fact that not only were these high-backed seats odd, they were incredibly uncomfortable. The rows were too close together to truly sit facing forward. It was as if twenty rows had been installed when there really only should have been sixteen. There was definitely a lack of knee room. I couldn't imagine anyone bigger than six feet and two quarters of an inch, one hundred and eighty pounds even fitting into the aisles. I thought of Jonathan Skew and hoped that his mansion in heaven was as unsatisfying as this.

After the first talk I got up the nerve to put my left leg up on the bench. Two minutes into the second talk I had worked myself up against the sidewall and spread both my legs out. By the end of that talk my head was leaning against the wall.

I was just opening a hymnbook to rest over my eyes so as to keep out the light when my attention was diverted by the appearance of a young woman at the opening of my pew. She looked at me and the position I was lounging in. She bit her lip and wriggled her left eyebrow. I should add that this woman was just about as beautiful as a person could get. She wore her dark hair long and down so as to accentuate her deep blue eyes. She was wearing a short white dress that magically seemed to speak forty languages all on its own. Of course, when translated all forty languages would be screaming, "Wow!" She was tan, but not so tan that one would think that she worshiped the sun in her off time. No, she was the kind of tan that suggested she spent an occasional afternoon working in her garden or reading to needy children on a blanket in a sunny park. She was . . . leaving.

I had been so struck by the sight of her that I had failed to realize that her blue eyes were searching for a place to sit. Of course I can't be sure, but it's possible that my being stretched out over the entire pew might have been the reason she continued searching for another spot. I wanted desperately to poke my head up above the pew and see where she had gone. I was scared, however, that she would spot me, and my awful first impression would be overshadowed by my creepy second one.

Before the final speaker, they called the ward choir up to sing to us all. I was hopeful about finally being able to see some of the members better, but unfortunately the ward choir consisted of only three people. Two of the members were women, an older one with big hair and uneven shoulders, and a younger one wearing a peach-colored shawl. It had been quite some time since I had seen a living person actually wearing a shawl—I felt so pioneer just looking at her. The third member of the choir was a man who had probably been told very early in his life that he had a nice voice. Sadly, puberty can ruin a perfectly good soprano.

It seemed like hours before sacrament meeting was finally over. At the conclusion I got up and tried to assess the crowd and maybe spot the girl who had caught me earlier. I hoped to catch her tripping, or with sleep marks on her face, so that we would be even in the Awkward Moment department. I could see no sign of her. I did notice, however, that there seemed to be a lot of members and that most of them looked to be around my age. This gave me a kind of hope I had not anticipated needing. I would have scanned more thoroughly, but I felt someone tugging on my elbow. I turned to find the formerly singing, big haired woman with uneven shoulders. She was smiling as if she were carefully following instructions on how to do so.

"I'm Sister Georgia Loft," she announced. "And you must be Andy."

"I am."

"We are happy to have you." Then she clapped. "Happy, happy!"

I hated to begin our relationship with dishonesty, but I figured she would respond better to a small lie. "I'm happy to be here," I said.

"I'm the Relief Society president," she informed me while shifting her uneven shoulders. "I know there's not a Sister Andy, but we still want to help. I'd organize a few meals for you, but since you're staying with Tat and Phil I'm sure you'll be well fed."

"I think that's true."

"Keep us in mind," she said, kindly patting my shoulder. "I'd like to think that we're in tune, but there are times when even I miss the signals God sends me."

"Thanks," I answered honestly.

"Do you know where we hold Sunday School?" she asked.

I shook my head, and she led me down the hall and left me alone in front of the Sunday School door. There wasn't anyone in the room yet and since I didn't want to accidentally take someone's usual seat, I decided to walk around the halls for a moment. The people I passed were friendly enough, but most just smiled at me as if they knew I was unfamiliar and they weren't sure that that wasn't the way they wanted to keep it. I spotted the bishop and made my way over to him. He shook my hand and asked me if I was who he thought I was.

"Why, what have you heard?" I asked suspiciously.

"Only that our new math teacher arrived yesterday."

We both smiled as if we were being funnier than we actually were. I told him that I was looking forward to receiving a calling, to which he replied, "We'll see what we can do."

The Sunday School class was fantastic. A sister by the name of Julie Ledbetter taught it and I had never seen such class participation or insightful instruction. She handed out little pictures of the Salt Lake Temple and told us that if we chose not to listen to the lesson that she would appreciate it if we would just stare quietly at the picture. I saw a few people in class taking her up on that. However, I listened, and I began feeling overwhelmingly happy to be there. I still had a lot of questions about the job I would be starting, but I knew I was going to get paid regardless of the answers. And yes, I was living in a pretty pink room on the top floor of the town's post office, but the bed was soft and Tat and Phyllis were friendly. I was just about to declare myself brilliant for making the move out here when I heard the classroom door open and someone hiss my name.

"Andy."

I turned to find Tat waving me over to the door. I stood up and slipped out.

"What is it?" I asked, once we were out in the hall. I was trying not to look too bothered. "I was really enjoying that class."

"I'm sure you were, but we've got a problem."

"What's up?"

"Just come with me."

Tat led me down the hall and out behind the chapel. Next to the giant anchor statue, out by the satellite dish and dumpsters, there were two boys and a middle-aged gentleman. I recognized the taller kid as the same paper boy who had wiped out in front of the Harding house—a huge bruise spread across his left check as a remnant of his earlier spill. Both he and the other boy looked mad about something. The shorter one had a live chicken in his hand. I could only imagine what the problem was.

"Bryan," Tat said to the middle-aged man. "This is Andy. Andy, this is Bryan Find." We both nodded.

"Andy," Tat continued, "Bryan caught these two boys out here fighting over this bird. Seems that they both think it belongs to them."

"Kids bring chickens to church here?" I asked.

"Chad here isn't a member," Bryan winked at me. His wink seemed to say, "together let's work to make him want to join the Church, serve a mission, and go on to further the work of this great kingdom."

It was a huge wink.

"Randall is the first counselor's son," Bryan went on. "He brought the bird to show his quorum. Chad here just happened to be around when Randall was retrieving him from the car."

"I was on my way to the pond," Chad said. "I've been raising and selling chickens so as to earn enough money to buy a new stereo."

"And you think the chicken belongs . . . " I didn't get to finish.

"I don't care what he says. It's my chicken," Randall said

defensively. "I named him Francis. I found him a week ago over by Knock Pond."

"She's not a chicken," Chad scoffed. "She's a hen."

"I know that," Randall snapped. "Of course it's not like I'm an expert on farm life like you. I do know that unlike ducks she doesn't like to be submerged underwater."

"You tried to drown my hen?" Chad huffed.

"No," Randall argued. "Besides, it's mine. Is your hen named Francis?"

I put up my hands. Not because I had something to say, but because I wanted them to stop talking so that I could ask Tat why in the heck he had brought me into this.

"Because you're a teacher," he said as if shocked by my question. "I figured that if anyone could solve this you could."

"Tat."

"Please, Andy," he begged.

I rubbed my forehead and moaned. I have never really figured out how or why revelation and wisdom come. I remember being invited to a party when I was sixteen. I prayed and prayed that God would let me know if it was the kind of party that a good Latter-day Saint boy should go to. It was an honest inquisition yet he never said one word. The lack of response made me curious as to why on so many occasions in my life when I felt I was doing just fine on my own he had thrown in a few words just to make my decisions harder.

Now, however, he seemed to be speaking to me right when I needed him to. It was as if I was finally on the same track. Or maybe it was the fact that it was Sunday and that it was Old Testament time on the curriculum circuit. Either way, as I looked at that hen I suddenly saw King Solomon and the solution that he had so wisely enacted.

"All right," I sighed. "Randall you think this is your bird?"

Randall nodded.

"And Chad you think she's yours?"

"I usually put duct tape around the legs of all mine, but it could have come off."

"Well, what I think would be best is if I just split the hen in half and gave a part to each of you."

They both looked at each other as my words sank in. I could see Randall's mind whirling a mile a . . . well, whirling.

Chad looked at Randall and shrugged. "That sounds good to me," he finally said.

"I'm happy with that," Randall agreed, handed me the unhappy bird.

The poor thing twisted in my hand as I stared at Randall and Chad in disbelief. "You realize that if I split her she'll die?"

"Can I have the top half?" Randall asked Chad.

Chad nodded.

Then everyone just stood there waiting for me to split the poor bird in half. I figured the only course of action was to call their bluff. I held the bird in front of me and pretended to tear it in half. I even made a semi-realistic ripping noise.

"That's not going to work," Chad said, shaking his head. "Here, use my knife." He pulled a pocketknife out from his pocket and opened it up. I took it reluctantly.

"The bird will die," I pleaded.

"Andy, I think you've done an adequate job of explaining that," Tat said, looking as anxious as the others for me to do the deed.

There was no way I was going to kill the hen. When I was twelve I had accidentally killed a bird with my slingshot. By "accidentally" I mean that I had aimed at it, but I had never thought I would hit it. My rock had hit him square on and the bird had tumbled from the tree landing smack dab on the plate of potato salad that was laid out on the park picnic table. I was so mortified by what I had done that I picked the bird up and hid him behind some bushes across the field. When I returned to the scene of the killing I found my parents eating the potato salad and asking me if I was having a good time. What could I say besides, "Yes," and, "I'm too full to eat anymore." It had been a traumatic event in my life. Now, I had a knife in hand and was supposed to finish off this poor hen. I decided to go for the calling their bluff tactic once again.

I slid the dull end of the blade across the bird.

"That's not how you do it," Chad complained. "Here give me the knife."

Before I could respond Chad had commandeered the knife and was thrusting his hand forward. I tried to pull the bird back but I was too slow. Blood squirted everywhere as I saw this poor hen's short life flash before my eyes. I could give a more detailed report of what happened next, but I feel it's sufficient to say that there was more blood, some screaming from the Primary class that had been meeting outside beneath the tree, and a strong feeling that I just might be in over my head.

CHAPTER SEVEN

UMM, UMM, ODD

Brigham Young only visited Thunder City once. Some felt that this spoke highly of them, suggesting that they were doing so well that they didn't need babysitting. Others worried that it proved just the opposite. The second theory seemed a bit more probable seeing how his one visit had turned out so disastrous. Plus, there was the tiny fact of him promising to never return. The one time Brigham had come he had addressed the Saints out in the large field that had at one point been the co-op farm. Taylor Lund wanted the prophet to give his instruction while standing on his section of the field. He might have gotten his way if it had not been for Orton Davis wanting the prophet to prophesy from his plot. The town council had an emergency meeting where the two men drew straws to see who would get the privilege of claiming that the prophet had stood on his ground.

Orton Davis won.

To show that there were no hard feelings, Taylor Lund volunteered his time making a portable podium on a flat wagon so the prophet could be seen and heard by all. When Brigham

Young came he began his speech on Orton's land but ended up somewhere else completely. The move was due to the low whistle commands that Taylor was sending to his horses who were hooked up to the pulpit. Orton started hollering when he realized what was going on, the horses got spooked, and President Young was never seen in Thunder City again.

After helping to cut a hen's life short I went directly home and to my room on the top floor of the Harding house. I tried cleaning myself with the sash Tat had let me borrow but it was no use. So, I just laid there on the pretty pink bed staring at my blood-soaked shirt and wondering just how I could get out of this mess of Mishap. I had wanted to experience the people of the West, but I had no idea that those people would be quite so interesting and uncouth.

I didn't move for the rest of the day.

Around six in the evening I got up and closed my window to block out the noise of Gordon and Tat playing Ping-Pong down on the back porch. I had never heard such a heated exchange of words over a game that consisted of tiny paddles and a little plastic ball. After I closed the window I lay back down and slept for a short while. I probably would have been out all night if it had not been for the loud knock on my bedroom door at around seven.

"Andy?" Tat hollered through the door.

Ignoring him didn't work.

"Andy?"

"Yes," I slurred, hoping to sound asleep and bothered.

I guess Tat interpreted my mumbling to mean, "Come on

in," because the door opened and he stepped up to the bed. He pulled out the cute wire chair from the desk and took a seat next to me.

"Hey, Tat," I said defeated.

"Something the matter?" he asked kindly.

"You were there," I said defensively, referring to the chicken incident.

"Life's complicated," Tat waved. "Besides, I thought it was a brilliant solution. Listen though, why don't you come down for some of Phyllis's cooking. I've known very few people that didn't perk up over the smells she produces."

"I'm not sure," I said, feeling the hunger in me coming alive.

"It'll do you good."

"She's not serving chicken is she?"

"Nope. She changed the menu just for you."

I sat up and handed him his sash. I then pulled off my bloody shirt.

"You know, Andy," Tat said looking away as if modesty was something he excelled at. "This city probably isn't at all like the one you just came from back east." He paused, acting as if he had given a lot of thought to the things he was now saying. "We do things differently here. But if you'll be patient with us you might come to see that we're not half bad."

"I've already realized that." I smiled. "I think it's going to require a little patience on your part."

"We're aware of that," Tat smiled back, his gray sideburns rising as he did so. "You have family back East don't you?"

"A mom and dad," I answered.

"Well, we'd better feed you so they don't get upset."

I put on a clean shirt and we headed downstairs. The dining room table was full of people waiting patiently for food to appear. Tat's daughter Sarah had a blanket draped over her, nursing her son, Markus. A nice looking older woman sat across from Sarah. She looked like she was straight out of one of those Church videos that had been filmed in the seventies. I remembered seeing her at church earlier in the day. An older gentleman, who I recognized from the ward as well, was blowing his nose into a cloth handkerchief while Phyllis busily ran back and forth from the kitchen bringing out food and filling glasses. I took the empty seat right next to Sarah Harding and her son.

"Andy's going to join us," Tat announced.

Phyllis stopped her hustling to smile. "What an honor," she said sincerely.

I waited for someone to introduce me to the others at the table, but Tat just started talking about other things.

"I tell you what," he told us all. "I was playing Ping-Pong with Gordon after church and he just couldn't say enough about what you did today, Andy. He thought your cutting solution was brilliant. Brilliant. You teachers have an answer for everything." Tat began scooping food onto his plate. "Phyllis, honey, mind if we pray without you?" he asked loudly.

I think it was hard for Phyllis to hear the question seeing how she was in the kitchen at the moment. Everyone bowed their heads. I kept mine up, figuring that I would keep a constant vigil on who wasn't closing their eyes.

" . . . For what we are about to eat let us be happy," Tat prayed. "And if sickness finds us, let it find us with time on our hands and a few days off. Bless the food that it might warm our stomachs and make us mellow . . . "

Eventually we all said "amen."

Phyllis stepped out just as people began raising their heads.

She put the last of the food on the table and sat down. We all began to pass things around.

"Eat up, Andy," Tat insisted.

"It looks delicious, Phyllis," I said.

"Thank you Andy, I— "

"My Phyllis is the best cook in town," Tat bragged. "I bet you've never seen a spread like this before."

"Actually, it reminds me of the meals my grandmother used to make," I said innocently.

"Oh really?" Tat questioned. "Well, did your grandmother ever make you snake gravy?" he challenged.

I watched Phyllis stab her first bite of food and lift it towards her mouth.

"I've never heard of snake gravy."

"Phil, honey, why don't you whip up a little of your famous gravy?"

Phyllis looked at her husband. Her fork was still full and her mouth was wide open.

"I'm all right," I insisted. "Really."

"Nonsense, Phil doesn't mind."

"Don't mind at all," she said, sounding very unconvinced. She got up and went into the kitchen. No sooner had the door closed when I began to hear pots and pans crashing and scraping as she whipped up her gravy.

"Leave a hole in your stomach big enough for a couple ladles of gravy," Tat smiled. "It's one of the last recipes that Phyllis still uses fetal in."

"Fetal?" I questioned.

"Fetal weed grows like hair around this part. I don't know that you can find the stuff anywhere else in the world," Tat said proudly. "Tastes terrific, but it does weird stuff to the nervous system. No one uses it anymore."

Another loud pan crashed in the kitchen.

"But Phyllis still puts it in her gravy?" I asked.

"Not enough to hurt. Oh, and Andy make sure you try some of her famous Triple Sour Pears there in the jar," Tat insisted. "Eat all you want; we've got a whole pantry full of them. Just don't get 'em too close to the candles."

The older Church-video lady picked up the jar of pears and handed them to me.

"Here you go," she said properly.

"Thanks . . ."

"Lilith. Lilith and Gary Stern," she introduced herself and the older gentleman next to her. "We're rooming in the large room on the third floor," she said. "Do me a favor, Andy, and don't be fooled by our last name," she smiled. "I can't speak for my Gary, but I'm easygoing and approachable."

"That's true," Tat said. "Lilith here is one of the most approachable and easy women in town."

Lilith blushed. "Thank you, Tat."

"Well, it's nice to meet you two," I said.

"Likewise. And listen, Andy. I sell Avon products so anytime you need anything you come to me. Now, I know what you're thinking—Avon is for women and women alone. Wrong." She made a loud buzzing noise that caused her husband Gary to jump. "Men can benefit from my wares as well. Do you have weak nails or a dry scalp?"

"Excuse me?"

"Brittle nails. Is your scalp flaky?" she asked.

"Really, I don't know . . ."

I would have gone on displaying my discomfort with the

discussion at hand, but Tat was up and staring at the top of my head.

"He looks okay, Lilith, but his breath . . ."

"My breath?" I asked defensively.

"Well, sitting this close to you I can tell that maybe your stomach's a little sour."

"Father!" Sarah stuck up for me.

"I can't hold back honesty," Tat insisted.

"You need to come see me, Andy," Lilith said with excitement. "I've got many products for the outer and inner self."

Lilith handed me her card as Phyllis came out of the kitchen and took a seat. The second that Phyllis began to lift a bite to her mouth a buzzer went off in the kitchen. She got up and left us again.

"You know, Andy, Sarah's been wanting to learn Spanish," Tat informed me while smiling at his daughter. Sarah blushed.

"That's great," I said, wondering what had brought this up and why he was telling me.

"She was hoping you might teach her." Tat chewed.

"I don't know how to speak—" I tried.

"She'll pay you. Sarah's just got herself a part-time job working with Ariel at the Photo Hut," Tat said waving his fork. "I don't know what Spanish lessons cost, but I assume they're not as expensive as English ones."

"Really, I don't know—"

"She used to have a job at the drive-in, but she quit for moral reasons," he explained further.

"Sleeveless uniforms," Sarah frowned. "I may have made some mistakes in my life, but it's not like I've got *stupid* tattooed on my brow."

Tat leaned over and scraped something off her forehead. "Just a bit of rice," he said.

Phyllis came back in and sat down.

"Phil, honey, is there more water?" Tat asked sweetly.

Phyllis got up and stepped back into the kitchen before I could even offer to help.

"So, Andy, tell us more about your first Sunday here," Lilith asked.

"There isn't much to tell. I went to church and participated in the slaughter of an innocent chicken."

Phyllis stepped back into the room and began filling everyone's water glass. Gary Stern finally added something to the conversation.

"I think the ward's getting too big."

Phyllis finished filling the glasses and sat down.

"I couldn't get a very good feel of how large the ward was due to the high-backed pews," I commented.

"That was one of Jonathan's extra touches," Tat said. He was talking with his mouth full. "He figured that there would be less talking and looking around if folks couldn't gaze anywhere besides up at the pulpit."

"There's been some great thinkers here in Mishap," Lilith bragged. "I don't think there are many places that have contributed to a better lifestyle than here."

I stared at her thinking she must be joking.

"That's true," Tat said. "Isn't that true?" he asked Phyllis as she lifted her first bite.

"Oh yes," Phyllis said sincerely. A light smoke began sneaking out from under the kitchen door. Phyllis put down her forkful of food and went to investigate.

"I'm not aware of what Mishap has contributed," I said

honestly. "Is there something about it that makes it different than any other Utah town?" I tried to say all this without sounding argumentative.

"Sure," Tat said.

"Of course," Lilith added.

Then they started eating again.

"For example?" I asked.

"Oh," Tat laughed. "For example, like the system of canals we have running into Knock Pond."

"Is that unique?"

"Well it works," Tat said.

"And we've got our carnival," Lilith added. "We've had folks from as far as Moab attending. This next one about a month from now should be our biggest ever."

"I can't wait," Sarah said excitedly.

"I can," Tat said, acting uncharacteristically sullen. "The carnival just brings in a bunch of rowdies. I think we should go back to the years when we used to have our Reverence Festival."

"That was so boring," Sarah said, rolling her eyes.

"Still . . . " Tat said.

"All those things are nice," I commented. "But they don't really make Mishap different. I mean . . . "

"Don't let them fool you, Andy," Gary spoke up. "It looks like no one but me has the guts to tell you the truth."

"Gary," Tat cautioned.

"The town has its problems," Gary blurted out.

"Now sweetheart," Lilith warned.

"I know we've all been instructed to act like nothing's the matter," Gary sniffed. "Tat here's worried you might get scared off and that we'd be lost without you."

"Me?" I asked in surprise, baffled by even being brought up.

"Yes, you," Gary insisted.

"Andy, why don't you have some more potatoes," Tat said, scooping more food onto my plate. "Don't you listen to Gary."

It was too late for that. Phyllis came back in and sat down in front of her food.

"What happens if I get scared off?" I asked.

"Phil, honey, don't you have something else Andy can eat?" Tat asked desperately.

Phyllis got up again.

"If you get scared off . . . " Gary began to say. I think a swift kick from his wife was what stopped him. "Owww."

"Sarah, why don't you take Andy into the living room and show him some family albums," Tat begged.

Maybe it was the threat of having to look at albums, or perhaps it was just my unquenchable desire to know what the heck they were all talking about. Whatever the reason, I decided to take a stand while remaining seated.

"What is going on?" I asked loudly enough to be taken seriously.

Lilith looked at Tat. Tat glanced at Gary. Gary smirked at us all. I heard Phyllis shuffling something around in the kitchen.

Tat sighed as if he were made up more of air than of matter. "I suppose we should tell you," he resigned. "Andy, not everything is perfect here in Mishap. We have been trying to make things look good, but Gary's right. We've got grief. What would you say if we told you that we prayed you here?"

"I'm not sure," I answered. "But I'd make a valiant attempt at not laughing."

"Let me just come right out and say it," Tat said. "Most of our young adults are too scared to marry. They're too skittish to say 'I do.' I don't know if you noticed at church, but we have an excess of single people who refuse to fall in love. A few have braved it, but even their example hasn't enlightened the majority."

Tat took a huge bite of potatoes. Not wanting to be rude by letting the conversation lag, he carried on as he chewed. "It's not that these kids don't want to. It's just that, well . . . "

"The town is cursed," Gary spat.

"What Gary means to say is that the spirit of what happened here with the Haps and the missing plane still seems to have an effect on us."

"That's *not* what I mean," Gary said. "What I mean is that old Harriet Hap's face showing up on the pond gives young folks the relationship jitters."

I thought of Lauren and sighed to myself.

"So the lake story is true?" I asked.

"Unfortunately, yes." Tat wiped at his face.

"Can anybody see her?"

"On certain nights," Tat answered. "The moon and weather have to be just right. We can't explain it. And we can't just pretend it doesn't happen. Too many people have witnessed her."

"I'd love to see it," I said honestly.

"You'll get a chance," Lilith replied.

"What do the experts say about it?" I questioned, wondering if they had brought in outsiders to figure out what had to be an elaborate prank.

"Now by 'experts' do you mean Ariel?" Lilith questioned.

"Who's Ariel?"

Sarah spoke up as if we had just introduced a subject she was quite fond of. "Ariel owns the Photo Hut. He has the best vision in town. I've seen him read a street sign from a mile away."

"I don't believe it," Gary sniffed. "What'd it say?"

"Stop."

It was a word I wish I could have applied to this conversation many sentences ago. I rubbed my forehead trying to make it look like I was just thinking really hard and not like I could feel a searing headache coming on. "So where do I come in?"

"You're going to teach everyone about how to have a successful and fearless marriage."

"You're kidding."

"Nope," Tat said, knocking his fork to the floor as he did so. "We figure we need someone to counter the presence of old Reinhold."

"He's still around?"

"Yep," said Lilith. "Poor soul just sits in his house and only comes out when it's dark or he absolutely has to."

"It's sad really," Gary added.

I was inclined to agree.

"Is he still the only non-Mormon in town?" I asked.

"Nope," Tat said with authority as he picked up his fork. "We had a small manufacturing business set up just outside of town about a year ago. That's brought a number of non-members in."

"We're changing," Lilith said almost mournfully.

"And we need you to help change things even more," Tat said to me. "We've tried just about everything else but still hardly anyone is jumping the gun to get hitched. A few have tried it. Take for example Cindy and Paul Bouwhuis. They got engaged just last month. But Paul mysteriously lost the ring, and Cindy suddenly noticed that Paul didn't like to watch iceskating as much as she did. Little things like that are keeping the curse alive."

"But that's normal," I said.

"Is it, Andy? Is it?"

Point taken.

"So you want me to try and correct all of this?"

Everyone nodded.

I couldn't believe it. The vague description of teaching a summer school class on relationships was actually going to involve dispelling a curse and helping a bunch of skeptical singles get married.

"I'm teaching marriage?"

Phyllis came back into the room and set a plate of steaming meat down in front of me. I was actually jealous of the roasted animal.

"I'm single," I pointed out.

"Then you should know where you're coming from."

"You know, I'm qualified to teach things like math."

"One plus one equals a couple," Tat said.

"This is unbelievable."

"We need you, Andy. We're willing to pay. We just think that as an outsider you might be able to convince a few of our less social kids that this curse thing is plain silly. My brother gave you the highest recommendation he could. I know you're the one." Tat showed Phyllis his dirty fork and she got back up and left us.

This was more than I had bargained for. "I can't do it." I shook my head.

"Please, Andy," Tat whined. "I'd hate to bring up the fact that you did sign a contract."

"To teach," I argued. "Not to marry people off."

"You'll be teaching."

"So if I instruct these students about relationships and stuff,

Mishap will pay off all my student loans?" I was double-checking.

"Every one of them."

I really didn't have anything to lose. Sure spending my summer convincing students that there's no such thing as a marriage curse and teaching people how to date was not what I was expecting to put on my resumé, but I could always just lie and say I had been on sabbatical to someplace unknown. And as much as this whole summer course deal had gotten out of hand, I didn't want to go back home and admit that I had messed up. Besides, for some odd reason I was beginning to like Mishap. I would have thought that maybe it was something in the water that was making me feel this way, but I had purposely avoided drinking any for fear of the very thought. Besides, to be completely awful and honest, there was a small, conceited part of me that thought I just might be able to help these poor folks out. Although I was single, I had done a lot of dating. Plus, I had read a number of Church-related articles on the subject.

"I guess I just need some time to adjust," I finally said. "This summer course is turning out to be more than I bargained for."

"Take all the time you need," Tat smiled. "The first class begins tomorrow at eleven."

I just stared.

"Enough talk about jobs." Tat slapped his knees. "I don't want to ruin a perfectly good meal by burying it with business."

I took a few bites and then politely tried to steer the conversation elsewhere.

"So they never found the plane?" I asked.

"Never," Lilith and Gary said in harmony.

"You'd think someone would have figured it out by now," I

thought aloud. "Or that someone would have come across the wreck."

"You'd sure think that," Tat said patronizingly. He reached for more food.

I'd have commented further, but a huge crash came from the kitchen. As the noise of it dissipated, I was suddenly struck by how calm the night was.

"It is awful peaceful here," I observed, referring to Mishap at large.

"These quiet nights are not unusual." Tat sighed contentedly. "We should have a peaceful season."

"Speaking of such," Gary perked up, "I sure do miss Summer."

"Me too," Lilith echoed.

I looked out the window. It was odd that they were talking like summer was over seeing how it was really just beginning. I figured that maybe they had some sort of different scale for summer here. Maybe because of farming or something it ended early out west.

"I'm always glad when summer's gone," I joined in. I had always liked the end of summer and the start of the new school year.

I got the feeling that those around me didn't enjoy outsider's comments about their seasons. Everyone just stared at me and squinted. Phyllis returned to the table and set a glass of what looked to be gravy down. She handed Tat his clean fork.

"What did you say about Summer?" Sarah asked me.

"I said, I'm glad when summer's gone."

Tat and Phyllis looked hurt.

"Our Summer?" Phyllis asked meekly.

"Your summer, my summer. Either way when summer's gone I'm happier."

"What are you saying?" Phyllis lamented, putting her hand to her heart.

"It's nothing really," I tried to explain. "I just get bored easily."

"How dare you," Lilith gasped.

"What?" I said defensively. "I enjoy summer but then I move on."

I would have said more, but Tat's fist in my face put a stop to my side of the conversation. I must admit, it came as a complete surprise.

CHAPTER EIGHT

YOU SAY TOMATO

I forgot you had a daughter named Summer," I apologized for the tenth time. I was sitting in Tat's parked boat out behind the Harding house and holding a bag of frozen peas up to my swollen nose.

"You're sleeping in her old room," Tat reminded me.

"Still, her name slipped my mind."

"These things happen." Tat forgave me. He cast his fishing pole out into the empty meadow behind his boat. I looked around at the night wondering if I had ever been any place more comfortable in my entire life. I could see a couple of people walking down the road near the river. One laughed. The tail end of a softball game could still be heard from across the large piece of land the Harding house sat on. I looked at the tall house silhouetted against the deep night. I could see into the kitchen through the window. Phyllis was sitting alone at the table, picking over everyone's leftovers.

"Sorry about the nose," Tat apologized.

"I would have done the same."

"Summer used to eat dinner at our place every night. I think Gary and Lilith miss her company more than Phil and I."

I sat up and repositioned the frozen bag of vegetables on my eye. I felt impressed to comment on the dry docked boat we were sitting in.

"I bought this after my father died," Tat explained. "My dad always wanted a boat."

"How far to the closest lake?"

"I suppose I could take it to Knock Pond, or there's a huge reservoir just above town. But what fun would it be boating without my father?"

Tat recast his line and an animal of some sort screeched. I stood up and set the frozen peas down. I then stretched like God must have intended men to.

"So you have only a mother and a father back home?" Tat asked.

"A great mother and father," I told him. "But yes, I'm an only child."

"That's too bad," he sighed. "I think big families are important. It would have been impossible to move that couch upstairs without Phil and the girls."

A truck pulled up to the side of the Harding house and what looked to be one amazingly feminine outline walked from the truck to the home. This well-drawn line talked to Sarah at the door for a brief moment and then left. As she turned, I could tell that it was the same someone who had caught me lounging in my pew. I watched her walk back to her truck and get in. The scenery I had been praising just moments before now seemed incomplete.

"Who was that?"

Tat turned from his latest cast. "Come again?"

"That girl. In that truck?" I pointed to the disappearing vehicle.

"That's Summer," he said in far too casual a tone for what he was describing.

"Really?"

"I promise," Tat smiled. "She went to Denver for school. It's nice to have her back here."

"I'm sure it is."

"We're pretty proud of that girl. You know, she's about your age. Maybe you could introduce her to some of your friends."

"I don't have any friends," I said, wondering how I could keep every other guy in the world away from her.

"That's a shame. You seem like a nice enough person." Tat cast his line out into the field again. The line whizzed and hummed.

I stepped down from the boat and told Tat that I was calling it a night. He made some sort of joke about how no sensible person would call it anything but that.

I climbed the stairs to my room feeling my spirits getting higher with each and every step. Right before I reached my door I noticed a thin red pamphlet sitting on a small hallway table. I glanced at the title wondering why I hadn't noticed it before.

From Thunder to Mishap: The Story of the Pinched Basin Saints.

I picked up the pamphlet and flipped through the pages, pausing to view an old photo or read a quotation. I was about to close it up when my attention was taken by the picture of a couple standing next to a plane. The caption below the photo read, "Larry and Tillie Cutler moments before their final flight."

I shivered for no reason. I looked away, looked back, and

then shuttered again. I felt the skin on the back of my neck rise. It was the most unsettling sensation.

"Odd," I whispered and closed the book.

I drifted to sleep with thoughts of aviation and Summer.

CHAPTER NINE

ADDED A PAWN

The subject of education was first brought up after Jerry Proudlock was attacked by a cougar that he had been throwing rocks at. Everyone wondered why Jerry hadn't simply known better. Thunder City decided then and there that they wanted to be known as a progressive, well-educated, and polished group of citizens. Of course after they realized all the work that status might cost they talked about settling for something less. "Less" being the reputation of having children that were at least smart enough not to throw rocks at cougars. It took a few years and one near casualty before they could begin to make such lofty claims.

I was by no means convinced that what I was doing was right in any sense of the word. I mean *me* teaching relationship skills to a bunch of people that were confused by folklore seemed sort of wrong. But on the other hand I was here, so why not?

I had always known that this year would be more interesting and curious than anything else. I had come west to do something different with my life and if teaching marriage prep to people more prepared than I was wasn't different, then I don't know what was. Also, if you promise not to tell, my entire life I had dreamed of being a superhero. I had grown up with Spiderman and Superman and an unquenchable desire to be just like them. More than once I had broken an arm or fractured a knee trying to fly or climb higher than the laws of physics allowed. Sure, I still couldn't shoot webs or fly so fast around the earth that I could turn back time. But I now had a chance to sort of step into Mishap and mend this injustice of what most likely amounted to no more than cold feet. I tried to think of a good name for myself.

"Captain Matrimony."

Our class was held Monday through Thursday in the ancillary building at Cornelious Thunder Community College. As far as my schedule, I had this summer made. After summer I faced one short year of teaching high school math and then I would be debt free and able to move on. I could bear almost anything for that amount of time. And Mishap, despite all the circumstances that surrounded me, was appealing.

I had written my parents before I went to bed the night before, so I put their letter in an envelope and dropped it off at the counter before heading out to teach. Tat was behind the desk sorting through mail.

"We got a little behind last week," he said, holding a letter up to the light. "Phil and I will be hitting it hard to get everything back up to speed. Oh, Andy." Tat sat up. "You got a letter from a girl named Lauren."

"You're kidding?" I asked in surprise.

"Nope," Tat smiled. "Apparently she wants to give things another try."

"How do you know that?"

It was a pointless question seeing how by the time I had asked it, Tat had handed me my open letter and envelope.

"You read my mail?" I asked incredulously.

"The seal was weak. I was afraid it might have fallen out previously and that the wrong letter had been stuck back in its place."

"Tat."

"I know it seems a few kilometers past the extra mile," Tat said flipping through more mail. "But you've got to understand, Andy, we look out for each other a little bit more than in those big cities."

"Thanks," I said sarcastically.

"Think nothing of it."

It was too late for that.

As soon as I was two steps out the door I pulled open the letter and read as I walked. Lauren had cooled down a bit but she was still not happy about me counting her out. She went on and on about our history and how we shouldn't just throw away our past like this. She brought up the fact that she was a staunch believer in love at first sight, and that even though she didn't fall for me immediately when we first met, she had since become convinced that love at first sight took time. She needed me. I felt bad, but not bad enough to change my course. In fact, I picked up my pace as I made my way over to where I would be teaching.

The community college was just about as small and quaint as a school could be without slipping to the lesser label of "dinky." The ancillary building was square and solid. There was a door at the front, a door at the back, and two window across from each other and on opposite sides. It had a flat roof and a flagpole out front that proudly flew the state flag up top and a city flag right below it. The flag representing Mishap had what looked like a gopher gnawing through a cliff wall with two stars over his head. I figured that someday I would have the courage to ask, "Why?"

I got to class early and spread out my few things in an effort to make it look like I knew what I was doing. Shortly before any students arrived, a thin, handsome man with dark red hair and an even darker mustache walked through the door. He had bony shoulders and pointed knees. His hair was a shade almost identical to the cliffs of Mishap at around five in the afternoon. This man informed me that he was a number of things. One: he was Pitt Frank, the Mayor of Thunder City. Two: he was married to Miss Pinched Basin 1994. Three: he didn't care for people that didn't take pride in their community. And four: he owned Franks Concrete and Gravel as well as more real estate than anyone else in town.

I thanked him for filling me in so completely and then asked if there was anything I could do for him.

"As mayor I run a tight ship, Andy," he said condescendingly. "I don't want you taking your eastern ideas too far here in class."

I swore that I would keep my eastern ideas to myself.

"I am not your enemy, Andy," he sighed. "I was all for you coming here."

"I can't thank you enough." I tried not to sound too sarcastic.

Heaven knows that I really didn't enjoy disliking a person until I had walked a mile in their shoes. But Heaven also knew that I was weak, petty, and selfish when the mood called for it.

So if I can judge for just a moment, Pitt Frank made me uncomfortable. From his gold-capped tooth to his incredibly hairy forearms, he unnerved me. His fiery hair and black eyes seemed to fit what I felt must be inside. A couple of times when he smiled I could see the polished expressions he was capable of—the expressions that must have helped him become mayor. But more noticeable than those expressions were the bad vibes that rose off him like steam from a thick, cheesy piece of lasagna.

"I am pro-growth," Pitt sniffed, pressing his lacquered look-ing mustache into his upper lip. "Thunder City won't reach its potential unless we promote a healthy lifestyle. Marriage will make us expand."

He had such a nice way of making something celestial sound cold and sterile.

"I'll do my best," I said, only because I felt that was what he wanted to hear.

"That's all I can ask," he replied. He pulled out a full-sized comb and brushed his mustache. I think he thought I would be impressed. He then nodded in a most calculated way and walked out.

"Nice to meet you," I said once he was gone.

At five minutes before eleven people began to arrive. I fig-ured that there would only be a few people with low enough self-esteem to actually show up to my class. I was wrong: every chair was filled. The last person in was Gordon. He stepped up to my desk and set an apple on it.

I thanked him and looked out at the students before me. What I saw was a class full of contemporaries. Everyone looked about my age or older. The girls in attendance looked like they had all begun experimenting with makeup that very morning.

The boys on the other hand appeared to have all used about a gallon of hair cream on their carefully parted hair.

"Welcome," I began. "I have to admit that this is a little awkward for me. I'm not far from your age, and I'm certainly no expert on marriage. But this should be a fun class. Who knows? Maybe we'll all learn a thing or two. I've taught for a couple of years now so I'll try to make this interesting and helpful. The book we'll be using is . . ."

A hand shot up in the back of the room and I pointed.

"My name is Nick Goodfellow," he reported. "I was wondering if we would be talking about things that were . . . well, you know things that . . . boy and girl things?"

"I think the answer is 'yes,'" I smiled, "seeing how this is a sort of marriage prep class."

He bit his lip for a moment in thought. "I'm comfortable with that," Nick finally said bravely.

"Good," I lied, looking at all those before me. "Maybe we should begin by telling each other who we are."

The introductions began in the front row and headed back. I was mildly interested in each and every person there. After all, I was the teacher and they were the students. But as each person stood and told the story as to why he or she was still single I had to wonder if God himself had the power to marry some of these people off. A few of them used their time for introductions to do little things that might distinguish them from the others. For example, Kell Tanabe made neat noises with his hands and then did an impersonation of Porky Pig saying "That's all, Folks!"

Jolene Thompson blushed until I thought she might pass out from an overdose of red. Sarah Harding went into great detail about her first failed marriage and how she didn't know if she could ever trust another man. Gordon stammered for a full two minutes and then told everyone about some of the specials at his store. A woman named Sylvia wearing dark glasses nervously introduced herself and then quickly sat back down. If I hadn't known better I would have sworn she was in disguise. Ariel Backer gave a discourse on how men should always use the terms *sir* and *ma'am* when talking to their elders. I think, although I really am not sure, he was simply saying this to prove to the women in attendance that he was very polite.

There was one married couple who had actually braved the curse of Mishap. They had signed up for the class in hopes of making what they had last. They were a young couple named Bert and Annie Lawson. Annie was pregnant and both she and Bert were miserable. I had never seen two people so stressed out over the responsibility of naming a child. No matter how they had tried, they claimed that they just couldn't settle on a name to label whomever it would be that did show up in a few months. Their fear was that they would pick something that others could tease or make fun of.

"If you have any suggestions we'd be grateful," Bert said.

"How about Marly?" Gordon threw out.

Bert thought a moment. "It's a great name, but I can just see kids teasing her by saying, 'Better safe than Marly.'" Annie looked at Gordon as if she couldn't believe he had even suggested such a cruel name.

After Bert and Annie, a girl named Debby Simmons introduced herself and then sang two verses of "When the Saints Come Marching In." At the conclusion she informed us that music made any mood better, and that perhaps with her voice she could break the curse of Mishap.

That was one theory.

Actually I felt as if everyone should be less concerned about a curse some harmless old man had uttered and more concerned about ending up just as they now were. I had never seen men and women have a harder time interacting. It was as if everything they had inside told them to keep apart from each other. Yet the moment someone of one sex turned away from someone of the other, the turned-from person couldn't help but look longingly. It would take more than a superhero to change this group. These people needed a prophet with the ability to part the gene pool.

About an hour into class, a dark shadow passed across the window behind me. I watched the entire class go pale. When I turned to see who was there, the window was empty. I turned back around.

"Are you guys all right?" I asked.

"It was Reinhold Hap," Ariel explained nervously.

"You're kidding," I said, walking to the window and looking to see if there was any sign left of him.

"He's not happy about all of this," Gordon said. "I heard he told Tat that this class would be the end of Mishap."

"Well, we'll have to prove him wrong," I said, trying to sound enthusiastic. I have to admit, I was a tad bit creeped out. It seemed as if the air in the room had turned stale simply by Reinhold casting his shadow.

"When you say, '*We'll* have to prove him wrong,'" Debby questioned suspiciously, "who exactly do you mean?"

"I mean us."

The class tried to be brave. I did my best to distract them from the feelings of Reinhold's appearance, but it wasn't as easy as one might think.

By the time our first class ended, I felt we had made a

couple of minor breakthroughs. In the last ten minutes of class, Kell Tanabe had finally stopped saying, "And that's the truth," in a funny voice after everything anyone said. And Ariel Backer had ceased calling all the women, "Ladies" and bowing towards them. Before I dismissed class I took a moment to read what the actual definition of a curse was—tomorrow I would hit them with the definition of love.

As everyone filed out, I suggested the name of Jeffery to Bert and Annie. It had been the name of my first dog and I couldn't think of a derogatory nickname that rhymed with it.

"Thanks, Andy," Bert said. "But I think it's just too close to 'hefty.'"

Once I was alone I straightened things up a bit and took a moment to realize that this wasn't going to be such a bad deal. I locked up the building and was in the beginning stages of whistling when I saw Tat pull up in his mail truck. He got out and waved at me as if we had a much closer friendship than the short time we had known each other could actually produce.

"Hey, Tat."

"Andy. Could we talk a minute?" He suddenly looked a little nervous.

We walked down through the trees and along a wide section of the Mishap water project. Trees above us shimmered in the wind, showing off their electric leaves. We talked about the weather and Salt Lake City. Then Tat asked bluntly, "How's Sarah doing, Andy?"

"Fine, I guess." I thought back to class and the few words she had actually contributed. "We're just getting started," I added.

"She's had a few tough knocks," he said. "I would love to see that girl stumble into something good."

"She's really a nice person."

"Listen," he said, looking around for prying ears. "I don't want you to do anything unethical, but whatever extra attention you could give her would be great. And although I'm above bribes, I can say with some certainty that you might find an extra scoop of potatoes at dinner or clean sheets more often."

"That's really not necessary," I laughed. "I'll help Sarah as much as I can."

"I knew you'd be good to her." Tat sighed, looking like the dad that every daughter didn't know she wanted.

A small part of me suddenly started to feel bad about not being more honest with him about how I truly felt. He was putting his trust in me, and I couldn't just play along blindly. That small bothered part grew until it was big enough to bully me into speaking.

"You know, Tat, I can't really convince any of these kids to get married," I said. "You know that, don't you?"

"Sure," he said skeptically.

"I mean I'll try to explain that marriage makes sense and how there is really no way that someone can curse a relationship. Or that if they get married they won't disappear in some mystery plane. But in the end if they can't just laugh at the legend and commit to someone there is nothing I can do."

Tat sighed. "No one's expecting a miracle, Andy. You have to understand, we just couldn't think of anything else to do. We've tried. Believe me, we've tried. But the problem is that we all messed up the kids too bad. When that plane went down our whole town went nuts. We were in shock. I thought with a little time behind us we could all move on, but the plane is still missing and that makes the curse seem ever looming. I know you probably think it's silly. But just getting all those kids together in a room like today gives me hope." Tat's sideburns flared as he spoke. He was a better soul than I gave him credit for.

"I'm here, so I'll try."

"Thanks, Andy," he sighed. "And about Sarah?"

"I don't think you need to worry too much about her," I said. "It seems to me like Ariel is a little fond of her."

"It's not a matter of *fondness*," he said seriously. "There is plenty of *like* going on. But no one wants to commit to liking someone for eternity."

We walked in silence for a few steps. I saw a little girl trying to fly a purple kite and an older boy rollerblading in an empty parking lot.

"Reinhold stopped by class today," I said, breaking the silence and watching for his reaction. He seemed unfazed.

"I thought he might," Tat said. "He's going to try to stop you, Andy."

"Stop me?"

"Like it or not, you're his new nemesis." I could tell Tat wasn't completely sure if he was using the word *nemesis* right. "Your presence gives him someone to hate more than Pitt Frank."

"You know, you could have mentioned that this job came with a nemesis when I first talked to you on the phone."

"Let's not get so tangled up in the little things that we miss the big picture," Tat said. "Let's look on the bright side."

"And what's that?"

"Well, you got a second letter from Lauren," Tat smiled. "She said she might come out and visit you sometime."

"You're kidding?"

"No, sir. Apparently she still feels for you."

"Tat."

"Things will work out," he comforted.

"So Reinhold and Pitt Frank don't get along?" I asked, hoping to cool down with a different subject.

"It's a long story," Tat sighed. "They were in business. Created some wonder paint with Willard Cutler. When Willard passed away it got messy. Reinhold and Pitt became bitter enemies."

"Pitt stopped by before class today."

"He said he might," Tat said soberly. "Pitt's a powerful man in this part of the state. Powerful man, Andy."

"I'm sure there's a lot of power to be had here."

Tat stared at me.

"I'm joking," I said.

"Actually, there is wealth here in this area. Pitt is proof of that. He and Reinhold were poised to make millions in that paint business if it hadn't fallen through. Pitt still has his gravel yard, and I'm certain he'll find other ways to get even richer. Unfortunately, he is also proof that money can spoil even the most preserved fruit. You can shellac an apple, Andy, but eventually rot is going to wiggle its way in."

"Well put," I said.

Tat beamed. "Nothing like a compliment from a teacher."

We had somehow circled back around to the ancillary building. Despite talk of Lauren I worked up the nerve to ask the question I had been wanting to.

"I noticed that your daughter Summer wasn't in class today."

"Summer won't show," Tat said. "She's got her new business to run."

"I'd be happy to tutor her," I offered, as we stepped up to Tat's mail truck.

"You are so selfless," Tat said seriously. "You know, I used to think that all easterners were snobby and conceited. But you don't seem that way at all."

I accepted the compliment without further comment.

"Will we see you at dinner?" Tat asked as he got in his truck.

"If not sooner," I answered.

Tat drove off without offering me a ride. I was happy he hadn't, seeing how I would have declined. I walked slowly through town looking at everything I saw as if it were the first time I had witnessed such creations. I liked where I was. I even liked Mishap's size. It was really a great perk that one could walk most any place they needed to. I thought of my old car that was still sitting in front of Gordon's store. I couldn't imagine ever needing it to get any place in Mishap. I loved looking for back roads or new trails to take me from here to there on foot.

I passed the huge gravel piles that made up the landscape and business Pitt owned. Each mammoth pile was a different color and made of different sized stones. The entire place looked like a tiny mountain range. I stopped and looked closely at all that Pitt owned. I would have been impressed if I wasn't so unimpressed by what he was actually like.

Just past Pitt's place I came upon Sylvia from my class sitting on a bench beneath a canopy of trees and staring straight at me. I would have just nodded and passed by, but her legs seemed to be blocking my progress.

"Hello," I waved.

"Andy," she said sounding nervous. "Could I talk to you?"

"Sure," I answered, seeing no very cordial way of avoiding it.

She shifted on the bench to make room for me. I sat reluctantly. She took off her dark glasses and stared. Having been taught early in life that staring was rude, I tried not to gawk back.

"Is something the matter?" I finally asked.

"You don't recognize me do you?"

"Sure I do," I said feeling a little confused. "Sylvia."

"Not from class," she pouted. "From North Carolina."

The pout had helped.

"Maggie?" I whispered in unbelief.

She smiled for a second and then stopped herself.

"I don't believe it!" I was completely in shock. The last time I had seen Maggie was right before I had thrown myself from a tree.

"I know," she said. "I couldn't believe it either. But when I saw you at church I knew it had to be you. You look the same, only grown-up."

"I had forgotten you moved to Utah," was the only thing I could think to say.

"I did," she said, as if I still didn't believe it.

"This is amazing. I . . . "

She held her finger up as if to quiet me. "I'm married, Andy." She said this as if I had been trying to steal her away.

"That's great."

She frowned. "I have three kids."

"That's great?" I tried.

She just looked at me.

"I'm tired," she complained. "And I'm not pretty anymore."

"That's not true," I said honestly.

"What's not true? The, 'I'm tired,' or the 'I'm not pretty?'"

"The pretty part."

"Thanks," she smiled.

"How long have you been married?"

"About six years," she answered glumly.

"So there are actually a few marriages that make it through the curse," I pointed out.

"Maybe ours has. But I feel awful, Andy."

"Why?" I asked. "Is he mean?"

"No," she said quickly. "He's a very sweet man. That's not it at all. It's just that, well . . . "

"Listen Maggie, maybe we shouldn't be having this talk," I stopped her. "I'm no expert. Maybe you should go see your bishop."

She started to cry. "He is the bishop."

"Wow."

"Can I still take your class, Andy?" she asked desperately.

"It's a community college," I said. "I don't think I can stop you. But you really should let your husband know."

"He's very busy."

"Maggie."

"I will."

I told her a few things about how nice it was to see her again and how it was just such a small world. She followed that up with a story about her youngest and how he was always biting the neighbor's cat.

It was a fair trade.

Before I headed home for the day I made a stop at the public library. For some selfless reason I desired to know a little bit more about Pitt Frank. It was just my luck that there happened to be an actual autobiography of him at the library. I stared at the cover for a few minutes before opening it up. The title was very impressive: *More Than Just a Man, More Than Just a Mayor: The Inspiring Story of Pitt Frank*.

By the time I left I knew more about Pitt Frank than any person should know about someone else—unless that person is looking for investment money or hoping to match up medically for the sake of an organ donation.

CHAPTER TEN

SAY CHEESE

The slow hand of the Wayne River had played a major role in creating the Pinched Basin area. Carefully and with much time, the water of the Wayne had given the land both function and mild esthetics. When Cornelious Thunder had first seen the place it was all he could do to not break down and cry. The open sky and barren landscape filled his heart with despair. He had left the comforts of Salt Lake City to make something out of nothing. For the sake of the company he had brought with him, however, he put on a brave face and refused to complain. When the barren winters refused to break, he prayed. When the hot summers melted the town's resolve, he fasted. And when a member of his own ward told him that his kids were unruly, he became offended, packed up his family, and left town for good. To this day there was not a single Thunder family member to be found within a hundred miles.

Tuesday's class went a little better than Monday's. Everyone really wanted to go around again and introduce themselves. So I had to break from the lesson outline and explain to them that they had grown up together and should be able to recognize each other by now.

Maggie came wearing her disguise again and sat in the very back row saying nothing. Bert and Annie were on a temporary high—thanks to the fact that they felt they had found the perfect name: Lisa. But then Debby Simmons pointed out that there was a famous painting that someone in Southern Utah had painted years ago called the *Mona Lisa*. And well, "Mona" was sort of like "moaning," and did they really want people moaning at their newborn baby?

Bert and Annie most definitely did not.

As far as relationships, I was encouraged by the fact that Ariel Backer and Sarah Hasting sat only five chairs apart instead of the seven they had the day before. Debby Simmons volunteered to sing the Ten Commandments for all of us. But I told her that even though I would love her to, others might not believe as she did. I had never been so thankful for separation of church and state. Jolene Thompson read a poem to the class entitled "Jolene." I'm not positive, but I think she wrote it herself. That or else some published poet out there had actually tried to rhyme the word *Jolene* with "warm spring."

Nick Goodfellow suggested that as a class we put together a "Tunnel of Love" ride for the carnival coming up in a few weeks. I told him that was a great idea provided he took on all the work himself. He thanked me for my permission and began scribbling ideas down on a piece of paper.

After class I found my camera and decided to take a few pictures of Mishap. I felt it was about time for my parents to see my new home. I also wanted to send a couple of pictures to Lauren. Her letter had been more needy than I had ever known her to be. In fact, she gushed so openly about us that I started to feel even more committed to the fact that the two of us should be over. Still, I owed her at least a letter. She had suggested that she fly down sometime in the next couple of weeks to visit me. I suggested that perhaps she should spend less time thinking about us, and that we should start communicating via E-mail so that Tat couldn't intercept everything we said.

I had had the same roll of film in my camera for the past year and there were still four shots left on it. So, I took my time walking around and deciding what the perfect four scenes to send home would be. For each one I got a local to snap the picture with me in it. In the end I felt pretty good about three of them. The fourth one had been taken with me in front of the Mishap mill, and I think I was blinking as it was snapped. I was surprised by all the historical places that Mishap had marked out for tourists. Apparently a lot of unknown and unappreciated Mormon history had happened here.

I walked down Angus Road and over to Main Street. At the corner I ran into a very hurried Pitt Frank. He tried his best to smile at me and then said time was money and at the moment he was broke. I smiled back, happy that he was destitute enough to leave me alone. I just didn't like him. Besides, I didn't need to swap words to know more about Pitt. Thanks to his autobiography, I knew more about him than he would ever know about me.

Pitt Frank's father had been an influential person in the Pinched Basin region—an influential person with an embarrassing first name.

His label was "Lilt."

Well, according to the autobiography, Lilt loathed his name. He tried many times to get folks to call him something else, but as much as he hated hearing it, folks seemed to enjoy saying it. It wasn't until Lilt beat the tar out of Lance Varney after he had thrown out a "Morning, Lilt," that everyone began to see things Lilt's way. Well, blame it on lack of creativity or just laziness, but either way everyone simply began calling him by his last name, Frank. So, when Frank married a few years later, Susan Wells became Mrs. Frank Frank.

Less than a year after they had tied the knot, the Franks welcomed their first child into the world. In tribute to the father they named her "Honor," as in "Honor Frank." Their second child was named "Blessed Frank" followed two years later by "Cherish Frank." Frank's self-worth soared as poor Susan continued to bring more little tributes into the world. Well, after "Thank," "Respect," and "Noble" were born, Susan became pregnant for what would be her last time. Sadly, she died giving birth to her seventh child. Suddenly Frank was anything but alone in the world. He had seven children and no wife to teach them how to be grateful for him. He took it upon himself to name the last child "Pity."

Pity Frank.

Well, everyone did just that up until the day Frank died. Shortly after his death all the Frank children, aside from Pity, flew the coop and left Mishap for good. Pity dropped the *y* and added an extra *t* for coolness. He also decided to stay and live off of the successful cement and gravel company that his father had built up. He remained, taking full advantage of his wealth and position by running for mayor. Pitt now lived with his wife, Keely, in the huge house that sat at the top of Wenton Road. I had seen both the house and the wife and in my opinion they were both more showy than I was comfortable with.

I put thoughts of Pitt aside and picked up my pace as I headed towards the photo shop. At the head of Main there was a huge cobblestone circle where cars could turn around or folks could walk and shop. On the edge of the circle sat a number of businesses. There was a T-shirt shop, a leather repair business, and a tiny photo shack that stood alone and back a few feet. I had never seen such a small establishment. It was no more than five feet wide and six feet deep. The top had a tiny wood-shingled roof and all four sides were glass on the top and metal on the bottom. I could see Ariel standing inside taking up almost every bit of room. I walked up to the east side and set my film on the minuscule shelf. Ariel jumped as if he hadn't noticed me.

Ariel Backer was a nice guy. He seemed like the kind of person that would fit perfectly into the background of anybody's pictures as an unknown passerby. He had light brown hair that in no way complimented his light brown eyes. In fact, if a person were to look at him through sunglasses they probably wouldn't even be able to tell that he had hair and eyes—those features would just get lost in the tint.

I slipped my roll of film through the small opening in the glass and told him I would like it developed.

"I suspected that," he said. "I'll need you to fill out this form."

The tiny shelf next to the hole made filling out the form almost impossible. I had to contort myself just to get into a position where I could actually write with the dull pencil that was attached to the short string. Amidst my struggles I almost didn't notice Summer Harding walking up to the west side of the booth. By *almost* I mean that she caught my eye much like a gigantic asteroid that was heading towards earth.

I was in awe.

"Hi, Ariel," Summer said from the other side of the booth. I could see out of the corner of my eye that she too was turning over some film.

Coincidence? I think not.

"Hey, Summer," Ariel greeted. "What can I do for you?"

I tried to get a better look, but I couldn't really see much of Summer due to Ariel blocking my whole view. I had never seen a skinny man seem so bulky.

"I'd like to develop this film. There's no hurry though," she said.

"I'm with a customer on the other side. Can you wait just a moment?" Ariel asked.

Apparently she was okay with this because he turned back to me.

"Do you think you could hurry it up, Andy? I've got someone on the other side."

"I can see that," I tried to say coolly. "Actually, Ariel, this is a really long form. Why don't you go ahead and help her."

"I'm okay," Summer insisted through the booth, having overheard what I had said.

"I'll hurry," I offered back.

Again she spoke to me through the booth. "You must be Andy."

Ariel turned around inside acting confused.

"Not you, Ariel," Summer smiled. "Him." She pointed at me.

Poor Ariel turned around again.

"And you must be Summer," I said, looking above Ariel's shoulder and over to her.

"I am."

Ariel leaned as far to the right as he could. He was still directly in the middle of Summer's and my conversation. He leaned to the left without any more success.

"You know," I said, trying to think up anything to keep our shallow conversation going, "I sort of feel like I already know you."

"I'm sorry," she laughed. "My dad loves to talk."

I would be lying if I said that I wasn't flustered. The bits and pieces I could see of Summer were like clues in a beautiful game of concentration. But with Ariel in the way, I just couldn't solve the puzzle. Not only that, but the form that Ariel was making me fill out to get my film developed was incredibly long and prying.

"Ariel, I'm not sure what my maternal grandmother's maiden name was," I said, pointing to line number twenty-three.

Ariel pushed his face up against the glass to see what I was writing. His right eye blinked slowly. It was not a pretty sight.

"You can skip that one," he said. "But make sure you answer the rest."

"So Andy," Summer said though Ariel. "I hear you're in my old room."

"I am," I said. I actually felt a bit embarrassed by the fact. "It reminds me of the one I grew up in," I tried to joke.

Ariel was lowering himself to give Summer and me a clear view of each other.

"You know we painted that room when I was ten," Summer said. "I always wanted to change things around, but Mom insisted that it stay the same. Even I feel a little silly when I'm in it."

"Maybe you're just not as in touch with your feminine side as I am."

Ariel stopped for just a moment to contemplate whether I had just said something racier than I actually had. With him stooped over, I could see Summer smile. I was worried about the light from her lips actually ruining my undeveloped film.

"So, how's your class going?" she asked.

"Fairly well."

I pushed my finished form though the slot, and Ariel raised back up quickly. He took the paper and looked it over slowly as if he were trying to spot some hidden picture on it somewhere.

"Do you want doubles, Andy?"

I nodded.

"We have a pay first policy," he informed me.

"No problem."

I took out my wallet and handed Ariel a twenty-dollar bill.

"Hold on a moment and I'll get you your receipt."

Ariel turned to Summer and asked her if she wanted double prints.

"Please. How much do I owe you?"

"You can pay me when you pick them up," Ariel whispered. "I just don't know Andy well enough to take the risk."

"Thanks Ariel," she whispered back. "It was nice meeting you, Andy," she said a bit louder.

"It was . . . " I started to say.

This was so stupid. Our entire conversation had been held through the booth. I couldn't let her go without at least getting a real word or glimpse in. I stepped to the side and over so as to be able to see her. It was a dumb move. She was remarkable. No, she was unremarkable. There was not a single remark in the English language that could properly sum up what she did to the scenery. She wore the smile of a woman that knew just enough as to not let on all that she did know. Her blue eyes were of a shade that even God couldn't name and her dark hair fell long and straight. And I hate to sound as if I'm shallow and two-dimensional, but Summer gave even the worst poetry body. She was a flash that didn't fade, leaving my soul blinded indefinitely.

"This is better," I finally managed to say.

"I agree," she said.

"Well, it was nice to meet you," I tried. "I guess I'll see you around?"

"It's a small town."

"Yeah," I said dumbly and as she walked off. In a few moments she was out of sight completely.

"She's something else, isn't she?" Ariel asked.

I could only nod.

"I don't think she's seeing anyone at the moment. Willis did say he and she were engaged, but no one really pays Willis much mind since that last camping accident."

I turned back to Ariel and he handed me my receipt.

"You know, Andy, I'd court her myself if her sister and I didn't have something going," Ariel bragged. "Well, that and the fact that she has turned me down more times than I can count."

"Sarah is a great person," I said, my heart not really in the conversation.

"She is. Of course, as you may or may not know we aren't actually going out, but I did just hire her, and I'm certain sparks will fly."

"Good luck," I said, selfishly directing my words more toward myself than him. I had a new mission in life. I didn't want to be Captain Matrimony anymore. I didn't want anything at the moment besides a chance to know Summer.

I couldn't wait to see what developed.

CHAPTER ELEVEN

TWO IS ALLOWED

In the early days of Thunder City people were prideful and arrogant. With their bright future and pleasant weather they seemed to have it all. At the heart of their pride was the fact that Cornelious Thunder had once informed them that Brigham Young had prophesied that someday they would all be looked upon fondly: that they would be viewed as the most chosen of God's people. How wonderful it was to have someone of such caliber pointing out the very fact they were already aware of.

Their arrogance might have risen to Zoramite proportions if it had not been for the letter that was discovered under the floorboards of Cornelious Thunder's old home. After the Thunders left town in an offended huff, a family by the name of Tart moved into their house. While the Tarts were building a bigger kitchen they discovered a box filled with old letters and a number of pictures. The photos told very limited stories, but the letters—now there was something. According to the fading ink, Cornelious Thunder had not been sent out to settle Thunder City because he had found favor in Brigham Young's

eyes. The truth was that Brigham had banished him from Salt
Lake City due to his heavy debts and a couple of inappropriate
things he had said to some influential local authorities.
Brigham had given Cornelious the worst part of the state as a
punishment. And Cornelious had the nerve to tell those he
talked into coming with him that they had been given the best.
To this day people still liked to imagine how perfect they would
be if only they hadn't been crippled from the start.

"She's only a girl," I told myself over and over as I walked
back to the Harding house. It was a technique I had learned
early on in life in order to prepare myself mentally for the let-
down that was certain to come. If I had ever needed prepara-
tion it was now. I mean Summer had smiled and laughed but
that was by no means her personal declaration that she had
heart and eyes for me only. I was suddenly mad that arranged
marriages weren't practical anymore and that my parents and
her parents hadn't sat down years ago and hammered out the
details involved in Summer and me living happily ever after.

Civilization had no sense of tradition anymore.

When I got back home I was surprised and frightened to
find Gordon up in my room spread out on a cot next to the
small white desk.

"What are you doing here?" I asked.

"Well, Tat and Phyllis got to thinking that you might need
a little company. So Tat suggested we room together for a short
while."

I couldn't believe this. "Really, I'm all right," I said.

"You can be straight with me, roomie."

"Gordon, this isn't necessary."

"No thanks is needed." He sighed like a martyr. "So what do you want to do?"

My life needed serious evaluation. Although I was intrigued by Summer and generally happy with the choice I'd made to come here, I couldn't just pretend that everything was perfect when deep down I knew there were some fatal flaws to my truly being happy here. I liked the people, but to be quite honest I liked the people I lived with in Charlotte. And even though I cared for the two groups in different ways I'm not certain that the ones I was now surrounded with were the ones I cared for more. I mean, I like simple and appealing, but those words are best suited in describing things like a child's drawings or the Sunday comics. Sure the town itself had some sort of weird pull on me, but I figured that came from the lady that appeared on the pond or the marriage curse that had downed a plane. These were interesting things in a *Ripley's Believe It or Not* kind of way, but they didn't really seem like characteristics one looks for while searching for a place to settle. Yes there was Summer, but back east there had been Lauren, and to the best of my recollection Lauren had already let me catch her. Summer, on the other hand, seemed a long way off.

"So what do you want to do?" Gordon asked again, interrupting my self-pity. "Want to take a walk or something? We could go pester Mr. Hap."

"You know where he lives?" I asked, my spirits liking the idea.

"Of course. Everyone does."

I had a sudden hankering to be like everyone.

CHAPTER TWELVE

IVY AND INTRIGUE

The afternoon had simmered and cooled. Light like foil fell over the town, shimmering in spots where heaven wished to find its reflection. A couple of lone clouds chased each other slowly across the sky only to break up and dissolve before either could declare a true tag. Gordon walked uncomfortably close to me as we strolled towards the Hap house.

"So did you grow up here?" I asked.

"Guilty."

"Do you think you'll stay here forever?"

"Why not?" Gordon reflected. "Can't think of something strong enough to pull me away."

"The world is bigger than Mishap," I pointed out.

"That may be true, but I don't want to know about it."

"That's a satisfying attitude," I teased.

"The less I know, the happier I stay." Gordon's big eyes seemed to be in direct contradiction to what his wide mouth was saying.

"Really?"

"Sure," Gordon insisted. "It seems like anything new always brings trouble. I'm okay with what's right here and now."

"But what about—"

"Don't want to know it," he interrupted. "Whatever you're going to tell me is only going to complicate things."

"That seems a little—"

"Don't say it," Gordon insisted. "Things seem fine to me and I don't mind them staying that way."

"So you're anti-change?"

He nodded.

"What about your store?" I asked. "You get new stuff in there all the time. You learn about new products and keep up to date."

"You'd be surprised."

He was probably right.

"Well, what about this marriage class we're doing?" I had him now. "Why not come to that? You might learn things that will change your life in huge ways."

Gordon stopped his walk and looked at me like I was crazy. "I might be against change, but I'm not against women."

"So women are the one area you feel you could change for?"

"I suppose."

"Seems like a rather boring life," I commented casually.

"I used to like hearing things," Gordon said. "Then my dad came home when I was seventeen and told me he was dying."

I wanted to crawl into the nearest gutter and cover myself with trash. I felt awful. I couldn't believe God hadn't warned me about this direction of discussion. Why hadn't heaven stopped me from bringing up a subject that was obviously still painful to Gordon?

"I'm sorry, Gordon."

"It's okay," he sighed. "You didn't know."

"I'm sure your father would be proud of you," I said, trying to comfort him.

"People say that," Gordon shrugged, "but I can't see how they can really know."

"I had a pet turtle die when I was seven." I don't know why I said it, but honestly, it was the only thing I could think to say. Gordon stared. "I took him out of his tank to play with him one afternoon," I foolishly went on. "I would put him in with my Lego houses and with my toy soldiers. I always pretended he was a horse or a tank. When my mother called me to dinner I hurried and cleaned up and then ran off to eat. It wasn't until the following afternoon when I got home from school and went in to feed him that I noticed the plastic truck sitting in the turtle's tank. I had rushed so quickly to put things away the day before that I hadn't noticed I had put the truck there instead of my pet. I found my poor turtle dead in the bottom of my bucket of Legos."

We walked in silence for a moment. Then Gordon said, "My father spent a month in the hospital and was in a coma for a week before he finally passed away."

I was the worst person in the world.

"Don't worry about it, Andy," Gordon said. "I'm thankful for what you were trying to say. I just think the only way I will ever try something new is if I'm shocked into it. And let's face it, there is less chance of that happening if I never learn anything new. So forget about it," he waved me off. "We can talk about something else."

I was thankful for Gordon.

"How about Reinhold?" he suggested for the new topic of conversation.

"So he's just the town hermit?" I said, relieved to have something else to talk about.

"He didn't used to be," Gordon said. "People used to love him. I always thought it was sad the way he ended up. Did you know that at one time he was almost a gazillionaire?"

"Really?"

"He was in business, with Pitt Frank and Willard Cutler. Larry Cutler's dad," Gordon clarified.

"What happened?"

"They created this wonder paint. Painted everything in town. A huge national company was interested in purchasing the formula, but then Willard died and took the secret to his grave."

"Pitt and Reinhold didn't want to sell?"

"They didn't know the formula. I guess Willard had kept it to himself. Pitt was pretty ticked off."

I was about to say something else, but Gordon suddenly stopped walking. I looked at him and then turned to face the direction he was staring.

I had seen unkempt houses before. In Charlotte there had been a neighbor not too many streets away who had decided he was tired of humanity looking at him so he planted trees over every inch of his property and let the bushes and grass grow tall and wild. He had even boarded up a few windows and fenced off his drive. That neighbor however could learn a few things from Mr. Hap.

The house sat like an architectural wart. Where there was earth, there were weeds. Where there was home, there was havoc. The roof was half gone and the windows were broken and black. I could see that the front porch was falling in and ivy grew over everything that would let it bond. What looked to be trash was scattered around liberally. A shoe was hanging from the sick tree that seemed to huddle over the house protectively. The entire place sent out vibes so strong and uncomfortable that I had to fight my legs to keep them from simply walking off.

"Someone lives here?" I whispered in disbelief.

"Mr. Hap."

"Have you seen him lately?" I asked, feeling like a twelve-year-old kid inquiring after the boogey man.

"Yes," Gordon whispered. "He buys stuff at my shop sometimes. He won't look you in the face and of course I'm not going to insist that he does."

"How old is he?"

"Probably sixty."

A light on the top floor flicked on and then faded away. The wind circled around the house and then over to us. I could feel my goose bumps protesting about me standing around.

"We should leave him alone," I said quietly.

"Everyone does."

Once again I was all too happy to be lumped in with everyone. I'm pretty sure we would have turned and left the scene without further complication if it had not been for the large thumping noise that came from within the house. The noise was followed by a low moan and the slamming of a door.

"What was that?" Gordon asked, grabbing my arm.

I wished that I had had the sense to visit spooky places with better-looking companions.

"I have no idea," I whispered.

Gordon turned to leave.

"What if someone's hurt?" I asked while stepping closer to the house. "Didn't it sound like someone falling or something?"

"We can't go around solving everybody's problems, Andy."

I ignored Gordon and walked across the overgrown yard and up onto the porch. I knocked lightly on the front door. I couldn't hear anything besides the nervous mumbling of Gordon who was still standing out on the sidewalk.

"Mr. Hap?" I called through the door.

Nothing. I tried the knob and it opened without protest. The stale smell of a closed-up home escaped out and over me.

"Mr. Hap?"

I stepped inside, leaving the door open for light. Silence blew up around me like a scent and made my skin crawl. I stepped carefully, the old floor pitching a fit about me walking around. A large green couch seemed to hiss at me—it scared me almost as much as the fat cat that bounded out from behind it. The yell I let out was not the most dignified.

"Andy, you okay?" I heard Gordon holler from outside.

"Fine," I hollered back. "Mr. Hap?"

I might have called his name a couple more times if it had not been for the pair of feet that I saw sticking out at the end of the far doorway from behind the stairs.

"Gordon!" I yelled.

He came far faster than I thought he would. I pointed at what I saw, and together we made the terrible discovery that Reinhold Hap was no longer with us.

Thanks to Gordon's high-pitched scream, within ten minutes the entire town of Mishap was either in the Hap home or standing out on the street in front of it speculating as to what had happened. Emergency personnel did their best to keep order, but Mishap was so accustomed to chaos that they could see no reason to calm down now. I retold the story of how I had come to find Reinhold at least a dozen times before those in charge would let me be.

I was more than happy to finally flee the scene. I couldn't believe that I had been so unlucky as to be the poor soul that discovered Reinhold. It crossed my mind that maybe Reinhold's death hadn't been an accident or from natural causes. But I couldn't believe that anyone within our boundaries had it in them to commit murder. I tried to forget about it and think of other things, but something in the pit of my stomach refused to let the subject die.

I wish things had been the same for Reinhold.

CHAPTER THIRTEEN

MOVED

In 1911, not long after the Thunder family had abandoned the very town they had helped settle, a man by the name of Buck Moore was elected the very first mayor. Not much was accomplished during Buck's term. In fact the only achievement he could honestly list was the signing of the Wayne River Water Project. Within the first few years the Saints had discovered that there wasn't quite as much water beneath their feet as they had originally thought. Wells seemed to run dry faster than they could be dug. Farms that had looked promising years before were now faced with the problem of no water. A Mormon architect from Salt Lake was brought in, and after spending a week surveying the town, he determined that it would be quite possible to establish a water system using the Wayne River to wet any and every spot the locals needed. It had been Mayor Buck Moore who signed the papers that got the project started. Four years later he was voted out and replaced by LeRope Hastle.

The town was pretty confused. Sure, that could have been a tag line to describe Mishap at any time of the year, but it fit now more than ever. Reinhold Hap was dead and as far as anyone could tell, nature had not been the one to shove him down the stairs. The theory that he had simply tripped and perished may have flown if it had not been for the fact that Gordon and I had heard someone fleeing the scene. Everyone was heartbroken by the fact that if that were the case then it was probably done by someone they knew. A number of officials had been called in from surrounding towns to help our authorities get to the bottom of this.

We were in a bad spot.

Tat, Gordon, and I talked long into the night trying to figure out who we thought could have done such a horrible thing. Tat's guess was that Harriet Hap had risen from the lake and finished Reinhold off. When I tried to explain to Tat that there was no such thing as ghosts, he simply challenged me to come up with a better explanation.

I couldn't.

I was happy when Bishop Hearth's secretary, Vinton Moore, called at around eight to set up an appointment for me to meet with the bishop later that night. It was weird, but I really had a hankering for a calling. And I knew that wouldn't happen until after I had met with the bishop. I was a little surprised by how late Brother Moore wanted to schedule my appointment, however. Brother Moore informed me that due to the bishop's job as a truck driver it was the only time he had available. He also asked me if I would meet with the bishop at his home to make it easier for him.

I had obviously agreed to those terms because I now found myself walking down Walfinger Street following the directions

I had been given to the Hearth house. Maggie and the bishop had a nice looking home. The front was long with seven windows and a uncentered front door. There was a mailbox next to the road that looked like a tiny barn and a brick path that lead from there to the door. I was happy to see that the porch light was on and that there were signs of life despite the late hour. I rang the doorbell and then stood back an appropriate two steps.

Maggie opened the door. I hadn't really talked to her since the day on the bench. She was dressed as if this was prom night and I had come to pick her up. I tried not to look surprised. She had smeared on green eye shadow and fixed her hair up in a mushroom-like hairdo. Maggie was tall and thin, and the long formal dress she had on displayed quite clearly that this was a woman I was standing before. The purple in her gown clashed horribly with the color of her eye shadow.

"Hey, Maggie," I greeted.

"Oh . . . Andy," she said, as if she had to dredge the recesses of her mind to actually recall my name. "I didn't know *you* were the bishop's appointment tonight."

"I am."

"Well, come in," she insisted.

"I'm not interrupting anything am I?" I said motioning to the way she was dressed.

"Oh, this old thing," she blushed. "I just put this on to do a little dusting."

I suddenly wished that I had followed the advice of all my Church leaders and never kissed a girl before I knew she was the woman I was going to marry. Because at this moment, that single kiss I had given Maggie all those years ago in that tree was looking to be more complicated than I could have ever imagined.

"Well, you look nice," I said kindly.

I think she giggled.

I was about to say that my friend had heard from her friend that her sister had told so-and-so that she just might like me, when Bishop Hearth mercifully emerged from down the hall and greeted me. Although I could tell he was a genuinely kind man, he seemed a bit oblivious to the fact that his wife was so decked out.

"Andy," he smiled. "It's nice to see you again." He ushered me into a small room that they were apparently in the process of converting into an office. There were wires sticking out of the wall and none of the fixtures or lights looked finished. I sat down on a chair in front of his desk. He sat, sighed, yawned, and then "wheewed." He looked tired.

"It's been a long week," he commented.

"Too bad it's only Tuesday," I tried to joke.

Bishop Hearth had probably been an attractive man five or six years ago. He had most of his hair and the remains of what could have once been distinguishing features. He was a couple of inches shorter than I and had me beat by at least twenty pounds. His eyes looked added on like an afterthought. They just didn't match his face. They were like round balls of wood that had been so heavily polished that all they could do was reflect.

"It's a shame about Reinhold," he sighed. "Sorry you were the one to find him."

I thought about saying, "Apology accepted," but I just kept silent and nodded.

"Enough about all that," he said. "Why don't you tell me about yourself, Andy." He leaned back in his chair.

I considered starting with the story of his wife and me in the tree, but I went with, "There's not much to tell. I was born in North Carolina, raised in North Carolina, and now I'm here."

"Family?"

"A father and a mother."

"Have you been a member all your life?" he asked as if he were trying to think up things to ask me. I figured I'd fill the air with words to give him a break.

"Actually no," I said. "My parents joined when I was three. So the heavens will have to forgive me for some of the wild and worldly things I did before I saw the light." My joke produced nothing but a slow, steady breathing from him. "Anyhow," I went on. "I have always wanted to see more of the West and this job seemed like a great opportunity to do so. I've had some great callings and some that really were challenging. But I'm looking forward to serving here in the Thunder City First Ward."

I think he nodded as if prodding me to go on. I say "think" because it could have just been a small jerk of his head as he was dozing off. I chose to look for the good in him by pretending that he was hanging on my every word.

"I've been out of school for a while and had a great job in Charlotte, but the school burned down almost two months ago. I suppose I could have found something eventually, but the prospect of moving here appealed to me. Funny, huh? I was teaching calculus when the school burned."

He now had his eyes closed, but he grunted as if he knew where I was coming from. Either that or he was having a dream where something funny had just occurred.

"So I'll be here for this year teaching math. Of course currently I'm teaching relationships," I kept going. "I don't know I'll do any good, but I like the students. It does make me a little uneasy, however. I mean since you're the bishop and all, shouldn't I turn the marriage prodding over to you?"

He didn't even grunt.

"Bishop?"

Nothing. I raised the inflection in my voice. "Regardless, I really hope that I can be a help in the ward," I practically shouted. His chin settled into his chest. "I'll serve wherever you need me," I hollered. "I'm temple worthy!"

He barely shifted. He was definitely out. I pretended like I was confessing a few major sins to see if by some chance he was still listening and I could shock him into consciousness. When I began to blush over my own made-up mistakes I stopped.

"Bishop?" I asked again.

Only deep breathing. I thought about walking out and letting him be, but Maggie was out there dressed in a formal and dusting. I cleared my throat. A soft snoring began. I recrossed my legs, purposely kicking his desk in the process. He didn't even flinch. I picked up a book off of his blotter and dropped it loudly. I was the only one who jumped.

I had no idea what to do. I sat there for a few minutes just listening to him breathe. I let the air get nice and still and then shook the entire desk with one quick shake. It didn't even faze him. I had never seen anything like it. Fear spread through my veins as I remembered he was a truck driver and the thought of the many hours he spent driving across our nation's roads. He could sleep through the kind of car accident that leaves entire towns devastated.

"Bishop," I tried one last time with my hands cupped around my mouth.

He had me beat. I probably would have just sat there until I dozed off myself if I had not spotted the long fluorescent light bulb that was lying on the carpet next to the wall. It was obviously a part of the renovation going on, but in it I saw a higher purpose. From where I was sitting I was easily able to reach down and pick it up. Then as if I were completely daft I reached across the desk and jabbed him softly in the shoulder with it as if it were a lance. I withdrew quickly, laying the bulb back down on the carpet. My actions had no effect. I picked it back up and poked again.

Nothing.

I couldn't believe I was doing it, but yet I picked it up a third time and jabbed him in the other shoulder. He sniffed a bit but kept on sleeping. I sort of brushed his ear with the metal pronged end of the bulb. He didn't even mumble. Finally I leaned forward in my seat and pushed the bulb hard into his right arm. I momentarily turned my attention from him as I changed my grip so as to be able to prod harder. It was while my eyes were distracted that he opened his. I don't know why, but he jumped at the sight of me jabbing him with a four-foot-long light bulb.

Some people are so sensitive.

His reaction caused me to loose my grip. The far end of the long bulb whacked against the corner of the desk and exploded into a million little pieces. Noise bounced around the room like an agitated monkey. Bishop Hearth fell back out of his seat as I flew to my feet and covered my eyes with my left hand. My right hand still held the jagged end of the ruined bulb. After a few seconds there was silence. Then came the sound of Maggie rattling the doorknob and demanding to know what was going on. She burst in and found her husband cowering behind his desk as I stood there pointing a broken glass tube at him.

"Stop!" she screamed. "I'm not worth it." We both just stared at her. "Andy, you shouldn't have said anything," she cried. "It will only make things worse."

"Maggie . . . " I tried.

"Burton," she interrupted me and ran crying towards her husband. "It was only one kiss. One kiss!" she wailed. "Am I not entitled to a simple mistake of passion?"

Burton Hearth looked more surprised than when the bulb had exploded. "What are you saying?" he asked in confusion.

"I love you, but . . . " She didn't have it in her to finish. She ran from the room like decent thoughts from a den of iniquity.

"Maggie!" he hollered after her. It was too late. She was gone. He turned his attention to me. "Andy?"

I set the end of the bulb down and tried to look innocent. I had always been a horrible actor. "I can explain," I said.

"It's true?" he said with confusion.

"Yes and no. What happened was years ago . . . "

He stopped me by simply pointing towards the door.

"Really—"

"Go," he said.

I had always been taught to support and sustain my local leaders. I saw no reason for now to be any different. I left on my own recognizance, but I felt more sorrow than someone who had just told his bishop that he had sold his birthright for a cup of chowder and half a sandwich. Just when I thought I could feel no worse, I remembered that I was sharing a room with Gordon.

I needed to change a few things.

CHAPTER FOURTEEN

PICTURE PERFECT

When the Wayne River Water Project was completed in 1917 the entire town rejoiced. Food was brought out in full force and games that made even children look childish were played. At the heart of the festivities stood the new pond. Water from the Wayne River ran into the big body of water and then split up into a hundred directions depending on what farm needed it at the moment. It was a beautiful thing to see. The pond not only gave the city H_2O security, it brought the place up a number of levels in the beauty department. The water that the Wayne poured into the pond was as clear as clean glass. And the clean, heavy soil of the area helped to keep the water spotless. There was not a single point anywhere in the pond where a person couldn't gaze from surface to bottom. A contest was held for the naming of the pond. After passing on a number of mediocre names they were forced to settle on a suggestion submitted by the mayor's daughter.

"Don't Knock It Pond."

Folks smiled until they were someplace where they could

properly rip it apart. Despite the majority's dislike of the name, it stayed. Nowadays, however, everyone simply referred to it as Knock Pond.

The first thing I did when I woke up was to phone the members of my class (except Sylvia) and cancel school for the rest of the week. I figured that it would be best for all of us to let the death of Reinhold get behind us. Every one of my students seemed extremely relieved that I was canceling. After I had made my calls I dialed up the bishop in hopes of explaining things. Maggie informed me that he had been up all night in a depressed funk. And that he had just left to head out on the road again. I said a quick prayer for every motorist from here to his final destination. When I asked her if she had told him that the kiss she had been referring to had taken place over ten years ago, all she said was "I was going to get around to it."

"Maggie!"

"I'll tell him, I promise."

I hung up and made my way over to the Photo Hut to retrieve my pictures. When I got there I saw that Ariel had Sarah Harding in the booth and was training her for her new job. It looked like some awfully tight quarters.

"Are my photos ready?" I asked through the glass.

"Of course," Ariel said defensively. "Sarah, could you pull up the pictures for Andy?"

I watched Sarah try to retrieve my photos. The small amount of working space caused her to push Ariel completely up against the glass. She found my packet and stepped forward, giving Ariel a couple of inches to pull back. Then, as she handed my prints to him, the corner of the pouch scraped his cheek. A long red line now connected his ear to his mouth.

"Your photos came out great." Ariel winked. "I took extra good care of you." Sarah shifted in the booth causing him to hit his head on the glass. "Summer just picked up hers," he added with another wink.

"Are you two okay?" I asked, wondering if he was actually winking or if he had developed a tick.

"Never better," Ariel said. He turned and elbowed Sarah in the face. She tried not to scream too loud.

"Sarah, are you doing all right?" I asked.

"I'm having a little trouble learning all the ropes," she smiled weakly. "But Ariel's being real patient." She reached up to retrieve something and undercut Ariel on the chin. He rubbed for a moment and then said, "Look, Andy, you're set. Just let me know if we can be of further service."

Sarah gave Ariel the one-two punch while waving good-bye to me.

"Are you sure you guys are going to be okay in there?"

Ariel leaned close to the glass and whispered, "Sparks are starting to fly."

If I had been a truly compassionate person I might have stayed and insisted that they needed help. But alas, I felt quite satisfied with my deficient compassion.

"Enjoy those pictures," I heard Ariel yell as I walked away.

I tried to shake my head in such a way as to not make him feel bad.

I waited until I was almost home to open my prints and look at them. I had always hated looking at pictures while others were looking at me. I think I was afraid that people might catch me smiling at myself. I could tell instantly that there was something wrong with my batch of photos. Instead of pictures of me doing stupid things, all I saw were pictures of Summer doing amazing things. Things like leaning against a rail, standing in front of a lake, and swimming at a beach.

I definitely wasn't smiling at myself.

I now understood what Ariel meant when he said he had taken good care of me. I would have thought him quite kind if it weren't for the fact that if I had Summer's photos she probably had mine. And whereas she looked better than fabulous in all of her pictures, I knew for a fact that there were a number of mine that could be used as proof that I was not completely competent. I changed my course and headed towards Summer's place. Okay, that's not exactly true. I slipped the beach picture out of the pack and into my jacket pocket and then changed my course and headed towards Summer's place. You can go ahead and judge me, but I feel it only fair to say that she had doubles and that I had always been rather appreciative of beaches.

I knew where Summer lived simply because it was a small town and there weren't too many places one did not pass in the course of living here. The front portion of her home was built to be a veterinarian's office. It was a cute place, with a wooden sign hanging from the front door that read "Dr. Summer Harding." I tried not to fault her for being pretentious. A green awning covered the big front window, and fading pink flowers grew alongside the walkway. Since it appeared to be a business, I opened the front door and entered the waiting room. There was a large fish tank in the corner and an old man sitting on a chair next to his black dog that was violently coughing. Summer stuck her head out from behind the office door to see who had just come in.

"Hey, Andy," she smiled. "Can you hold on a moment?"

"Sure," I smiled back. "I'll just sit here and look after your fish."

She disappeared. I took the only available seat left. Unfortunately it was the seat right next to the choking dog. The moment I sat down his cough became worse. His owner seemed undisturbed by it—in fact, it looked as if he were asleep. I couldn't believe how tired everyone in this town was. I tried to focus in on something else besides the coughing dog but he turned his head and began to drool on me. I tried to politely push his head away, but every time I did he simply moved back into the same position.

"Excuse me," I said, trying to get the owner's attention.

He didn't answer me. I tried again to push the dog away but he just kept on drooling and coughing. I stood up just as Summer came out with a young boy who was holding an orange cat with a swollen face. She said a few nice things to the boy and he left. She finally turned her attention to me.

"So what are you doing here?" she asked nicely.

"Actually, maybe you had better take care of these two first," I said, pointing towards the coughing dog. He drooled as if on cue.

"They can wait. Besides, I think he's faking it," she joked. "So what's up?"

"Well, I went to get my photos today, and I think I accidentally got a couple of yours."

The dog coughed again.

"What a coincidence; I got a few of yours as well. Come with me," she said, waving me back. We walked through her office and into what looked to be a living area. Summer picked up my pictures and handed them to me.

"Here you go."

"I'm not sure I want mine back," I said.

"Oh, I don't know." She smiled. "This one's particularly cute." She showed me the one where I was standing in front of the city mill and blinking in a most unbecoming way.

"I can explain."

"I'm sure you can," she said, holding out her hands.

I reluctantly handed her the pictures. She set them down without even flipping through them. I suddenly felt really bad about keeping one for myself. So bad in fact that I said, "Well, I guess I should be going."

"Right," she smiled. "And I've got a drooling animal to attend to."

I'll try to say this in a dignified and respectable way. Summer Harding was an outstanding individual. I wouldn't have been surprised in the least to learn that some dignitary somewhere had just named her "Miss Everything." She was one well-kept secret. I just couldn't let myself walk out without asking.

"I know it sounds dumb," I said. "But would you like to have dinner sometime?"

"Dinner?"

"I'd offer dinner and a movie, but since this town only has a drive-in, I'd better save that experience for a really special night."

"That sounds fun."

"Really? It won't creep you out to go out with some guy who is sleeping in your old room?"

"I'll try not to think about it."

"Tomorrow night then? About 6:30?"

She smiled. I knew when to exit. I said a couple pleasant

things and then hightailed it out of there before she could change her mind. I couldn't believe how easy that had been. Perhaps Mishap was a more charming place than I had given it credit for.*

CHAPTER FIFTEEN

WHIP SNIP AWAY

F ashion arrived in Thunder City on May 1, 1934. It came in the form of Sue Faye Melton opening a small beauty salon in one of the empty stalls in her family's barn. Patrons sat on bales of hay while Sue Faye snipped and styled anybody that would submit to her hands. Her clientele soon moved beyond the type that felt comfortable sitting on straw for hours at a time. Needing to step up or fade out, Sue Faye talked David Nuckols into letting her use a small corner of his hardware store in exchange for free haircuts for him and his family. David Nuckols jumped at the chance. He made room for her by moving his hammer section back behind the lumber. He then began hinting to his wife that they needed to have more kids seeing how the value of his deal increased with each addition to their family.

Sue Faye cut hair there for many years before she was able to afford her own building. When she finally passed away, the family let Sue Faye's nephew Whip take over. He was probably the wrong person for the job, but he needed something to do.

≡ ♥ ≡

It was with very little forethought that I decided to get my hair cut before my first date with Summer. My hair was longer than it needed to be and there was a small barbershop right off Main Street. The two facts seemed to need each other. Besides, I had heard that the barber was a brother of Larry Cutler—as in Larry and Tillie and the missing plane. I was dying to ask him a few questions about his disappearing sibling. True I could vaguely remember Tat telling me something about having Phyllis cut my hair because Whip Cutler was a little different. But I had found that barbers that were a little different seemed to do a good job. Besides, it seemed a bit too intimate to have Phyllis cut my hair. I just wasn't comfortable with someone who cooked most of the food I ate touching my head for such a long period of time.

I made my way over to the barbershop and walked in. I had never seen a cleaner haircutting establishment in my life. I wouldn't have been the least bit uncomfortable having my gall-bladder removed or my heart operated on in such a sterile place. The whole room smelled of cleaning solution. I looked around at the two empty haircutting chairs and the mirrored walls. A small, shining sink sat silent in the corner. At the front of the shop sat a slight man on a tall stool. He had a neat mus-tache and wore a white smock. Everything about him was slight and pointed. His ears peaked, his lips pressed together sharply, and his nose seemed to poke annoyingly at the air in front of his face. The name tag on his uniform clearly said "Whip." I closed the door softly behind me, feeling as if I needed to be reverent.

"Hello," I whispered.

"Hello," he said back.

"I was hoping to get my hair cut."

"Okay," he smiled.

I stepped towards one of the empty barber chairs, but he stopped me.

"If you'd please have a seat in the waiting room. I'll get to you as soon as possible."

I looked around at the empty shop. The waiting room was a single chair next to the front door.

"Is there a long wait?" I asked.

"Not too bad," he said. "Ten, twelve minutes."

I took a seat on the lone chair. There were a couple of magazines but I found it hard to read them with him just sitting there staring off into the distance. The ticking of the clock helped make time feel incredibly slow. I cleared my throat a few times hoping that would help speed the wait along.

It didn't.

Finally after about seven minutes he stood up and walked over to the far wall. He took a comb out of some blue solution and began to examine it. He looked at it slowly and then blew on it a couple of times. After that he pulled out a cloth and thoroughly wiped the counter above where he had blown. I felt my skin begin to crawl. It was as if time had actually stopped. He shuffled over to the west wall and straightened the two pictures hanging there. That needless task completed, he returned to his stool and sat. I couldn't take it any longer.

"Are you waiting for someone?" I tried to ask kindly.

He just laughed as if I had told a halfway funny joke.

"No, really. Is there someone you're waiting for? Because I wanted to get a few things done before . . . "

I stopped talking due to the fact that he looked wounded by my words.

"I don't mean to be pushy." I tried to soften my approach. "I would just really appreciate it if . . . "

He stood and said defensively, "I didn't realize you were in such a big hurry."

"Well, I just want to get done so . . . "

"Enough with the pressuring me. I've had a really stressful day—two cuts and a styling. I was just trying to settle my nerves."

"I'm not pressuring, I just wanted . . . "

He put his hands up over his ears as if to block out what I was saying. As soon as he realized that I wasn't going to say more, he took his hands down and pointed to one of the barber chairs. I moved to the chair and he put a dark green cape around my neck and started right in on my hair.

"Would it help if I told you what I wanted?" I asked.

"A haircut, right?" He said it as if challenging me.

"Right," I said, frightened into submission.

Three snips into my mystery doo I felt and heard a tremendous sneeze on the back of my neck. I turned my head only to be turned back by the hands of Whip. I wasn't going to say anything, but he sneezed again.

"Are you okay?"

"Fine," he said, moving my head back into place. "Haaawcheeew!"

"Really," I insisted. "Could I get you a tissue or something?"

"No need."

I begged to differ.

He snipped for a few moments and then moved around to the front of me. I don't think I had ever been more scared. I tried to put my hands up in front of my face so that just in case he sneezed again I would be covered. But the cape I had on made that more difficult than I would have liked. I was trapped.

He sniffed and then sneezed to the side of me.

"Maybe I should come back." I winced.

"I'll be done in a minute."

He shifted to the side.

"So Larry is your brother?" I asked, hoping to talk him into stopping his sneezing. I would have thought that he was ignoring me if I hadn't been able to see him nod in the mirror on the wall.

"Do you have any idea what really happened to him?"

I didn't know Whip well enough to know if a sneeze meant yes or no.

"Bless you," I said, somewhat disgusted. "Where do you think the plane is?"

Either there is a place called "Huuuupshhhip," or Whip had finally found the courtesy to sneeze into his sleeve.

"That's just awful about Reinhold," I changed the subject.

He showed his grief by sneezing three rapid sneezes.

"Listen, Whip, why don't I come back and have you finish the rest later."

"That'd be silly." He blew his nose.

"But drier."

He laughed as if he actually got what I was talking about.

"Heeeeewaaassp!"

"Honestly, Whip," I pleaded.

"Just a little hair allergy."

"But you're a barber."

I think he thought I was complimenting him. I tried to stand.

"Just a moment more." He jerked my noggin back in line. A couple more snips and "All done." He held up a small mirror so that I could see the back of my head. I looked a lot like most of my male students.

"Would you like some gel?"

"I'm fine," I said.

He sneezed twice as I was getting up and three times as I was trying to pay. I think I gave him a twenty-dollar tip just because I wanted to get out of there. The moment I was free I ran my fingers through my hair and cursed Tat for not going into better detail about why a person should avoid Whip's place.

It took me two showers to feel clean again.

CHAPTER SIXTEEN

TABLE FOR THREE

I n 1941 a miracle happened in Thunder City. Farmers planted their crops and prayed that God might make the harvest bountiful. God did just that, giving the settlers something to look fondly upon as harvest time drew nearer. But before a single kernel or stalk could be harvested, a horrible thing occurred. From out of the river that ran through the bottom of Pinched Basin came frogs—thousands and thousands of frogs. They overtook the settlers and their crops. It wasn't so much that they gorged themselves as it was that they were so fat and in such numbers that their presence laid waste to any field they hopped through. The Saints were devastated and frightened. In their hour of need they managed to gather and pray fervently to the heavens for relief. Winter was coming and without the planned harvest the young town would surely starve. God's answer didn't come written on a scroll or stone tablets. No, the answer came when a young man whom the town called Mule discovered that with the help of a skewer and a warm fire those frogs didn't taste half bad. Mule McLaughlin wasn't the sharpest tack, but his hearty appetite had sparked his gray matter into finding a solution.

The town commenced collecting and smoking three cellars full of frog. Next summer when the frogs ran out, heaven found the town fat and more convinced than ever that God cared for them personally. To this day, a statue of a heavy frog sits at the center of Thunder City as a reminder of the blessings of being a Saint and of the possibility of miracles.

It wasn't easy to convert the haircut I had received into something that I felt comfortable walking around with. But eventually I got it so that I could at least look myself in the eye. I stressed about what to wear for my first date with Summer but ended up feeling decent about what I settled on. The white shirt and Levis were just neutral enough to make a statement.

I tried to pace myself as I walked to Summer's place because I wanted to arrive at just the right moment. Once there, it took me a few minutes to decide whether I should ring her office door or walk around back. I took the back way. I knocked once. Before I could think about knocking again Summer yelled at me through the door.

"Just one second, Andy."

Three seconds later she opened the door to give me a full view of what I was up against. My outfit was all wrong. Of course anything I could have chosen would have been all wrong when held up next to her. But her blue eyes reminded me that it wasn't the clothes that made a woman, and her smile let me know that she was happy to see me.

"You look wonderful," I said, a little more dazed than I would have liked.

"Thanks. So do you."

"You must not have looked closely at my hair."

"I heard you gave Whip a try."

"Best haircut I've ever had," I joked.

She smiled. I felt it was the perfect moment to offer her my hand—she must have agreed because she accepted the offer. I wasn't sure what would be the best place to eat seeing how I hadn't tried too many places. So I let location be the determining factor and took Summer to Heidi's Italian restaurant. It was located just down the street from her place and consequently required minimal footwork. I had thought about getting my car for the night but I hadn't moved it since I had originally parked it in front of Gordon's place and I still wanted to leave it that way. Besides, I had tried to start it up yesterday afternoon and it wouldn't catch. I figured it at least needed a jump before it would be running anywhere again.

The restaurant I chose was dimly lit. Its floors were covered with carpet that looked thicker than the lies my uncle Herman used to tell to my aunt Jane. The moment we stepped inside, a young skinny man with perfectly sprayed hair and tiny glasses popped out of the back room and greeted us.

"Good evening. My name is Tim. How are you two doing?"

"Fine thank you, Tim," I said cordially.

"You two are quite lucky. You just missed the dinner rush. Every table is available for you to chose from." He swept his arm across the empty restaurant.

"We'll take your best one," I said, handing him a five-dollar bill.

"Absolutely," he winked with enthusiasm. "Right this way."

Tim seated us at a small table in the middle of the restaurant. I personally didn't feel that it was really his best one. Actually I don't think there was a best one, seeing how all the tables in the place were extremely close to one another. He handed us our menus with flare and then asked, "May I take your order?"

Summer and I glanced at each other and smiled.

"Would it be all right if we took a couple of minutes to look over the menu?" I asked.

"Sure," he waved. "If you need me sooner, just give a holler."

"Thanks," Summer said for the two of us.

I had been expecting Tim to walk off into the back room, but instead he dropped into a seat at the table right next to us and flipped open what looked like a planner. He was so close that it was almost as if his back was sitting between us. Summer and I looked at each other and tried not to laugh. We then made a valiant attempt to discuss the menu.

"So have you eaten here before?" I asked her.

"Its been awhile," she answered. "I think the last time was about a year before I left for school. Of course back then it was called Kim's Pancake House."

"So you have no real recommendations?"

"The pancakes were good."

"I don't see those on the menu any longer," I said, pretending to scan it.

We looked and, "Hmmmed," for a few moments.

"I think I'll have Heidi's Alpine calzone," she decided.

Tim began tisking as if she had chosen poorly. We both stared at his head as he sat there with his back towards us. Summer spotted a new menu item of interest.

"Maybe I'll try the sweet and sour chicken," she tried.

Tim "ahhhhed" as if she had chosen wisely.

"I guess I'll have that as well," I conceded, feeling as if it would be best to just go with the crowd.

I was expecting Tim to jump up and start taking our orders but he just continued to sit there flipping though his planner and penciling in dates.

"We're ready to order," I finally said with feeling.

Tim looked over his shoulder and spotted our closed menus. He couldn't have jumped up any faster.

"Ready to go?"

"We are," I said. "I think we'll both have the sweet and sour chicken."

"Excellent choice. And to drink?"

"Water's fine," Summer said, spreading her napkin on her lap.

"For me too."

He took our menus and then finally left us alone.

"Is that normal?" I asked, referring to Tim's almost joining are party.

"You didn't want him to sit by us?" she smiled.

"It's just that . . . "

Before I could finish my response, Tim returned with a tray carrying three glasses and a plate of food. He gave us our water and then set a glass down on the table he had been sitting at earlier. He set a plate of food next to his drink and then sat down and began to eat rather noisily.

"You're not concerned?" I asked, trying to be vague enough that Tim wouldn't know I was talking about him.

"Maybe a little."

Tim's food smelled delicious. Good enough that I figured it would be worth hanging on for ours.

"So, did you always plan on settling back here in Mishap?" I asked, deciding to pretend that he just wasn't there.

"Not always." Summer sipped her drink. "But I came to realize there are a lot of things I missed. Besides my family is here. How about you? Do you like it?"

"I can think of one thing I really like." I whispered so that Tim wouldn't hear. He leaned his head back as if to better eavesdrop.

"Really," Summer smiled. "And what's that?"

A bell went off in the kitchen and Tim ran back to check on it.

"Should we move to a different table?" I asked.

Before Summer could answer, he was back out with our food. He ceremoniously placed it in front of each of us. I'm no gourmet chef, but the meal didn't exactly look like it had been made from scratch. In fact, I could still see the shapes of the TV dinner tray compartments it had been dumped out from.

"Will there be anything else?"

"No, I think we're fine," I answered dishonestly.

"As I mentioned before," he said sitting down, "if you need anything just holler."

We started in on our meals doing our best to ignore the fact that Tim was practically sitting between us.

After a couple of bites I asked Summer, "So what do you think about this marriage curse?"

She swallowed and said, "I try not to."

"I mean it's sort of silly that I'm teaching this class." I wiped my chin, took a drink of water, and continued. "I almost don't feel honest calling what I do work."

"They wanted you to," Summer insisted, putting a little more emphasis on the word *they* than I would have preferred.

"So by *they* do you mean not you?"

"No offense, Andy, but I wish we could have gotten over this fabricated fear without having to offer a college course on it."

"None taken."

"You know, I'm glad you're here."

"Well, it wouldn't hurt to show it every once and a while," I joked.

She put her hand on mine. She smiled, giving me a glimpse of what heaven must have intended teeth to look like. It actually took effort to stop myself from leaning over and kissing her. Well, effort and the fact that Tim was in the way. Summer lifted her glass and drank the last of her water. I did the same, wanting to be just like her.

"Excuse me," I said to Tim. "Could we get some more water?"

"That'd be great," he smiled. "Just grab that pitcher over on the table. I'm almost empty as well."

I figured what the heck. I stood up and retrieved the pitcher. I then filled everyone's glasses. Tim gave me a half-hearted thanks. I put the pitcher away and sat back down.

"So what do you think happened to Reinhold?"

"That's another thing I don't like to think about," Summer said. "It's horrible. We've really shown how open we are to non-members."

"You don't know it was a Mormon that did it."

"Have you looked around, Andy?" Summer motioned. "There's pretty much nothing but Mormons here."

"Still," I tried.

"You sound just like everyone else who refuses to believe that one of our own has done something so horrible."

We both took a couple of bites in silence.

"So what do you think happened to the plane?" I asked.

Summer looked at me and shook her head. "You're really curious about that, aren't you?"

"Don't you think it's fascinating? I mean a plane goes down between point A and B and no one can find a trace of it."

"They probably flew off to get away from this place. Who knows? They might be living happily in some other part of the world."

"That doesn't make sense," I said. "They left everything they have here. And according to their family no contact has ever been made since they disappeared."

"Then they crashed in some dense forest."

"And no one has ever discovered it? That seems impossible."

"Maybe Mishap is like the land version of the Bermuda Triangle," Summer tried. "Things just simply disappear. In fact someone said that Sister Clovis lost her good wheelbarrow at the ward cleanup day."

"I heard the deacons quorum went on a joy ride with it and then tossed it down in the west canal," I said glumly, completely unsatisfied by her lack of serious interest in this.

"Andy, I know you think this is some fascinating mystery, but here it is just life." She was trying to comfort me. "A bitter old man threw out a hollow curse and a young couple accidentally helped him look prophetic. From all I've heard, Larry Cutler wasn't the greatest pilot. The plane crashed in some overlooked spot and someday someone will stumble upon it. And that will be that."

"Not really," I insisted. "If the plane ever is discovered it still doesn't discount the curse. I mean the Cutlers did die in marriage. But I don't really care about that. I am just interested in where the plane actually did go down. Or if it really did."

Tim coughed a couple of times to get our attention.

"Yes?" I asked. "Do you need more water?"

"Actually, I was thinking that if you could hand me that dessert tray over there, I'd be able to go over our specials."

"I think we'll pass on dessert."

He held up his hand and motioned for me to lean closer to him.

"You're going to look cheap if you don't order dessert," he whispered. "And having just ordered water isn't helping your case either. I'm only trying to help you out."

"Would you like some dessert?" I asked Summer.

"No thanks, I'm fine."

"She doesn't mean it," Tim whispered. "All girls say that."

"Tim says you really want dessert. Is that true?"

"He is the expert," Summer laughed.

Tim smiled with pride.

I gave in. "I guess we'll have some dessert."

"Great," Tim motioned. "The tray is right over there."

I stood up and got the dessert tray. We looked over the three selections for a longer period of time then was actually necessary and then decided on the chocolate cheesecake.

"We'd like to order this one," I pointed.

"Great. Just go right ahead and take it."

"Aren't these the samples?" I asked.

"No, no, that's our desert tray," Tim smiled.

"Don't you shellac these things to make them last?" I questioned. He answered me by leaning over and taking a selection from the tray for himself. He then took a gigantic bite of what looked like carrot cake.

"It's delicious. Take a bite," he prodded.

I pulled the cheesecake off the tray for Summer and me to share. We each took a small bite of it. It tasted like pulpy chalk that had been soaked in spoiled raisin pudding.

"Delicious," Summer complimented.

Tim smiled.

I forced myself to swallow what was in my mouth. "Well, I'm full," I falsely confessed.

"Me too." Summer set her napkin over the stale dessert.

"Suit yourselves," Tim said.

We did just that, leaving on the table what had to be more than enough money to cover our tab and getting out as fast as possible. We waited until we were out of hearing range and then laughed until it was hard for me to catch my breath.

Thunder echoed in the distance and spots of lightning flashed.

"That was the oddest meal I've ever had."

"I don't know," Summer smiled, pushing her long dark hair back behind her ears. "The company wasn't all that bad."

"Are you talking about me or Tim?"

She looked at me out of the corner of her eye. I couldn't see her mouth at the moment, but the way her left ear rose I knew she was smiling.

We walked in silence back to her place. Only the sound of protesting thunder broke the still of Mishap. I walked her up to her front door where we stood beneath the awning. Summer fished through her purse for her keys.

"I thought people didn't lock their doors in small towns," I commented. "They never did in Mayberry."

"I don't remember anyone in Mayberry ever getting murdered."

She found her keys right as it began to rain. The awning was not quite big enough to completely cover me.

"You're getting wet," she pointed out needlessly.

"I hadn't noticed." How could I with her standing there?

"I'd invite you in, but my parents warned me about teachers."

"I'll just stand here then." I don't know why I said that, seeing how it was a complete and utter lie. I pulled her closer and kissed her before she could say anything. She kissed me back in such a fashion that I had no doubt about her liking me. The rain ran down my back and I could feel each particle of my being pause as if to pay tribute to God and the miraculous fact that he created both woman and man.

Summer pulled back just enough to say, "Andy."

I had never been so happy to be me.

We were so engrossed in each other that we failed to notice an old woman who had walked up and was now standing right next to us.

"Oh, brother," she griped. "While you two stand there slobbering over each other my sweet Nimble is giving birth."

Summer pulled away. "Right now?"

"Yes," the woman snapped.

"Who's Nimble?" I questioned, feeling a need to be included.

"Nimble is my horse," she said proudly.

"Can I help in any way?" I asked, thinking back to what possible TV show I might have seen in my life that would have prepared me in some way to help deliver a colt.

"Oh, no," the woman said. "I don't want any hanky-panky going on while my innocent Nimble is making miracles."

I felt inclined to tell her that I agreed.

"I'll call you tomorrow," Summer said and smiled. She then

gave me an abbreviated version of the kiss I had gotten earlier. Before I could say anything the two of them had walked away leaving me standing there alone in the dark.

I took my time walking back home. The rain seemed to fill the air with even larger amounts of oxygen than usual. I took a little detour so as to be able to make the night last longer. I would have pronounced my life perfect right then and there if it had not been for the thin figure that stepped out from the trees and called me by name.

My hope was that it was some underfed angel who had come to bless me further. But the truth was just the opposite— all except the underfed part. Pitt Frank had found me again.

"Pitt." I greeted him as rain fell lightly on us both.

"I thought we should speak," he said.

"Here?" I asked, looking into the rain.

"I'll make it quick. I don't think this arrangement is working."

I was wondering what we had arranged.

"What do you say we pay you, and you just make your way back home," he suggested.

"I take it you don't mean 'home' to be the Harding house."

"You're as perceptive as Tat claims."

"Why should I go?"

"Let's just say I think we need to solve this problem on our own," Pitt purred. "No offense, Andy, but you aren't one of us."

Up until his last few words I hadn't thought about things feeling wrong. Now, however, I was incredibly uneasy and upset by him telling me that I should leave.

"I think I'll be staying a while longer," I said firmly.

"I don't think so."

"We have a contract."

"Things have changed," he argued.

"I want to teach, Pitt," I said firmly. "I like it here. Besides, I want to find out what happened to that plane." I said it nicely, hoping to lighten the mood.

"The plane shouldn't concern you," he said sharply. "It is no mystery. Those two went down because Reinhold Hap predicted it."

"I don't believe that, and I don't think you do either."

"How dare you!" he spat, or maybe it was the rain.

"No offense, but his curse is silly."

"I don't like you, Andy," he said suddenly calm. "I don't like the fact that you've come here thinking that you can help us."

I know that Pitt was older than I was and that I should have been giving him my respect, but he had the personality of a Russian doll. Every time he spoke it was as if he popped open to display a tinier, less impressive version of himself inside. I didn't like him or feel that I should give him my time. Actually, I didn't want to give him anything but a fat lip at the moment. The mood just seemed right for throwing a few punches.

"I can see you're getting angry," he verbally poked.

It was the perfect thing to say. I was so set on him not being right that I was willing to simmer for the sake of him being wrong.

"Good night, Pitt," I said.

He said something vulgar and then tried to make an impressive exit. He would have been closer to accomplishing that objective if it had not been for him bumping his head on a low branch as he turned to leave. Frustrated, he swore again and made a poor attempt at salvaging any sort of an impressive anything.

I walked around for a little while and then took some time

to just sit on the small wooden bench that was safely dry beneath the awning of Whip's barbershop. I watched the rain fall and wondered for a second if it would be possible for a person to count the drops. The wet night kept Main Street relatively pedestrian-free. A woman in a huge truck drove by and a teenage boy emerged from the electronic shop across the way and locked it up for the night. He walked off whistling.

By the time I finally got home, the night had already started in on a new day.

CHAPTER SEVENTEEN

ASLEEP NO MORE

When Reinhold Hap first arrived in Thunder City he brought with him the trade of a painter. He could paint anything perfectly—any color or any shade. His steady hands worked miracles with a bucket and brush.

Reinhold's dream was to create his own line of paints from some of the local flora and materials. But he struggled with some of the complex formulas needed to invent paint that would actually hold up under the elements and conditions of Utah. Just as he was about to shelve his dream, Willard Cutler and Pitt Frank agreed to become partners with him and help out in the few areas where Reinhold lacked. Pitt put up the money and Willard came up with a formula that held up regardless of what you did to it. They called it the all-purpose paint, and together they painted everything. They made a killing—coating the street signs, storefronts, billboards, and cars. Shortly after they had painted the very plane that was now missing, Willard Cutler expired due to a heart attack. Reinhold and Pitt would have continued painting, but Willard had kept

the formula a secret from both of them. Unsatisfied with anything less, Reinhold laid down the brush and had not touched it
since. The partnership broken, Pitt focused his attention on his
other businesses.

The glory of those high times was never achieved again.

I was surprised by how much our ward was affected by the
death of Reinhold Hap. With Bishop Hearth out of town on
business, Brother Crammer called for a sort of impromptu testimony meeting. Everyone got up and tried as hard as possible
to let their brothers and sisters know that they were not the
guilty party. They also all stressed that they had absolutely no
connection to anyone who was.

I bore my testimony largely because I wanted to see if I
could spot Summer's head out in the crowd.

No luck.

Maggie bore her testimony and burst into tears as she began
listing the things she was thankful for. I tried not to make eye
contact with her for fear that she might list me as one of the
positives. When she didn't, I began to wonder what was wrong
with me.

Sister Georgia Loft, the Relief Society president with the
uneven shoulders, bore her testimony while simultaneously
giving out compassionate service assignments to a few of the
sisters in the audience.

Tat got up and said a few things about family and faith and
small miracles that were constantly nipping at his heels and beg-
ging to be noticed. I wanted desperately to look around and see
if the rest of the ward was as moved as I was by what I was

hearing, but all I could see was the Tart family to the left and the deep, rich wood of our awful pews.

Tat thanked the heavens for his two girls and his single grandchild. He admitted that even at his age he still found Phyllis cute. He then let those in attendance know how grateful he was that I had come around.

I had never realized just how smart Tat was.

When I tried to thank him after the meeting for the nice things he had said, he simply gave me his standard, "I can't hold back honesty."

I felt compelled to hug him or something. I went with a really watered-down version of the "something" by patting him lightly on the shoulder and then quickly walking off.

I saw my first small miracle that Tat had been talking about when I walked into Sunday School and noticed that Ariel and Sarah were sitting only two chairs apart from each other. The lesson began strong, but in all honesty I have no idea how it ended. I fell asleep halfway through it. I remember my eyes growing heavy sometime during the discussion about makeup and immorality. I tried acting like I was simply being spiritu- ally reflective instead of sleepy by closing my eyes. The next thing I knew, however, I woke up to find myself sitting in a dark and almost deserted room. I wish I could have said that I was there alone, but there were two other members in different spots both sleeping.

Something was not right in Mishap.

Even though I was surrounded by closed eyes, I couldn't remember ever being more embarrassed. I got up and slipped out of the room and into the hall. The last hour of church was just getting out and folks were beginning to emerge from class- rooms and preparing to head home. I spotted Summer four doors down talking to Peggy Tart, the Thunder City public librarian. Peggy had thin hair, deep eyes, and a pinched expression. She was nodding her head as if Summer had just said something she could really, really relate to. I didn't want to interrupt, but I felt compelled to get as close to Summer as possible.

"Hello, Andy," Sister Tart greeted.

"Hello." I tried to supress a yawn.

Peggy Tart yawned herself. She finished what she had been saying before I interrupted and then walked off. My plan had worked: I now had Summer all to myself.

"Where have you been?" she asked me.

"I fell asleep," I said with embarrassment.

"Where?"

"In Sunday School."

"Are you all right?" She laughed.

"I'm not sure. What is it with this town and everyone being tired?"

"I think it's just life," Summer answered.

"It's more than that."

Summer wanted to talk about other things. So, I gladly indulged her, but my mind was not with her one hundred percent.

Something was not right in Mishap.

CHAPTER EIGHTEEN

HAP HAZARD

"Have you heard?" Tat asked as I came down the stairs the next morning and caught him working. He was wearing a brand-new cowboy hat and a faded T-shirt that read: Stamp Out Disco.

"I don't think so," I answered.

"They called in the big guys from Salt Lake to see if they can't find out what happened to Reinhold."

"That's good."

"I don't know," Tat said reflectively. "Mishap's never taken kindly to strangers poking around."

"It's a murder investigation," I pointed out.

"Still."

"You don't really want some ne'r-do-well running around do you?" I asked.

"Like I've told you before, Andy, I only know English."

"Actually what they should do is go talk to Pitt Frank for a few minutes."

"Why?"

145

"It just seems like he's not very broken up over Reinhold passing away."

"He's a private man," Tat said defensively. "He's probably hurting inside." Tat switched tracks. "Oh, you might want to check your P.O. box. Lauren's written you again."

I pulled my key out of my pocket and opened up my box. It was empty.

"There's nothing here," I said closing it back up.

"Oh, that's right," Tat laughed. "I've got it right here." He lifted up his paperweight and handed me a folded out piece of paper.

"Did it come like this?"

"Andy," he said, as if I were teasing.

I ignored him and read.

> Dear Andy,
>
> I've made a decision. I will be flying into Salt Lake City on the twenty-first. I think that it would be beneficial to our relationship if we could spend a couple of days evaluating our future. As Gonzala Heratio once penned, "Love finds those who peek when they're told not to." I think that says it all.
>
> See you soon,
> Lauren
>
> P.S. I'll be wearing that red shirt that you like so much just in case you've forgotten what I look like.

I couldn't believe Lauren wasn't giving up. I also couldn't believe she still liked Gonzala's poetry. Why couldn't she just let our relationship die? I had been pretty straight about how I felt and where I saw us ending up. Now just as I was beginning a relationship with Summer, Lauren was insisting on barging in and making things even more complicated than they already were. I glanced at the calendar on the wall. The twenty-first was only five days away. I considered calling Lauren and insisting that she come to grips with reality. But then I thought that maybe I should just let fate run its course. I decided it might be a good idea for her to come out and see that I was doing fine on my own. Maybe this needed to be settled face-to-face once and for all.

When I got to class, no one was there yet. I puttered around and then emptied the wastepaper basket. It wasn't until the clock showed twenty after that I realized no one was going to show. And it wasn't until thirty after that it occurred to me that the death of Reinhold probably had a lot to do with everyone's absence. I had thought the time off would have been all that was needed for everyone to come to grips with what had happened. It looked like I was wrong. I locked up the place and walked over to Gordon's store. My car was still parked out front and Gordon was behind the counter looking through a hunting magazine.

"Hey, Gordon."

"Hey, Andy."

"I guess you couldn't find anyone to work for you so that you could come to class."

"Actually," Gordon replied, "Jeff could have come in but I thought I'd just work. I'm not too sure that I want to be thinking about dating and stuff anymore."

"Really?"

"Yeah. Seems like a dangerous time to be falling in love." Gordon's balding head turned red at the mere mention of love.

"Is that how everyone else feels?"

"I can't speak for . . . well . . . yes."

"I guess I should just pack it in," was my try at reverse psychology.

"You gave it your best," he said.

"So you'll never marry?"

"Let's face it, Andy. My chances weren't great before the curse."

He had a point.

"It's hopeless," Gordon sighed.

I suddenly wished that I could have done something to help. I had failed as Captain Matrimony. Gordon was destined to live out his life as a lonely clerk.

"I'm sorry about all of this," I said.

"Don't worry about it. If it'll make you feel any better, Nick is still going to go forward with the tunnel of love he's working on for the carnival. He's going to put up a tent over the west canal and just have everyone float through on inner tubes. It should be real romantic."

I didn't want to comment, so I dropped the conversation and walked across the street to speak with Tat. After I filled him in on my deserting class and what I saw was a hopeless cause, he told me to hold on and then ran off. A couple of minutes later he was back and informing me that the Council of Seven would be meeting tonight and that they would like me to come. The way he said it made it sound like it was too great an honor to pass up.

"Why do they want me there?" I asked.

"That's not as important as the fact that they *do* want you there, Andy. It's a rare thing for an outsider to be invited, but we trust you."

"We?"

"The council. The very people that brought you here."

"Is all this necessary?"

"It's your future."

"So they'll be deciding my fate?"

"Makes you feel important doesn't it?" Tat smiled.

Summer had already told me that she would be busy tonight. So I saw no harm in meeting up with the famous Council of Seven. After all, it could prove entertaining and had a certain element of intrigue.

"Where do we meet?" I asked.

"I'll show you." Tat smiled slyly. "Just be here in the foyer at ten."

"Why so late?"

"Pitt doesn't even close up the gravel yard until eight. I mean come on, Andy, it's not like the council doesn't have day jobs."

I took that as my cue to leave him to his. I spent the rest of the afternoon walking around town and thinking about Reinhold Hap and the missing plane. For some reason, I felt that the answers to the plane's whereabouts were tucked somewhere deep in my gray matter. It was a weird feeling, but I just knew that if I could trigger the right thought I could pull up the solution that had been there all along. I walked around the Hap house a number of times and spent a few hours at the public library looking up everything I could find on the Cutler's fateful flight. I stopped by Whip's place and asked him a few more questions. I even talked to a few of the out-of-town cops that were still poking around for answers.

I ate dinner at the Brick Red Café. It was a nice dive tucked back behind Finch's Hardware and Home Improvement. The food was great and in talking to the waitress I discovered that she had dated Larry Cutler before he became engaged to Tillie.

"I'm sorry about the accident," I said.

"He's not dead," she commented casually while refilling my drink.

"How do you know?" I asked. I was excited.

"I liked Larry," she sighed. "We had a connection. I would have married him if he weren't so pale. Anyway, I used to get these impressions when he was sick or needed something. He broke his wrist once and I knew it before he phoned to tell me."

"How'd you know it?" I asked, biting into my sandwich.

"My wrist started swelling."

"Wow," I said, about both her comment and the sandwich.

"If Larry had died I would have felt it," she insisted. "Besides, I still get impressions of him."

I was very happy that I had picked that particular place to eat. By the time I got back home it was past nine and Gordon was already tucked in his cot waiting for me to arrive.

"I didn't know if I should go out looking for you," he said protectively.

"You made the right choice not to," I joked as I took off my shoes and sat down on my bed.

"Hey, Gordon, have you seen my watch?" I asked, remembering that I had been unable to find it earlier in the day. I wanted to wear it to the council.

"Nope."

"I'm also missing my black belt," I informed him.

"Oh sure, blame it on your roommate," he said offended.

"I'm not blaming it on anyone. I was just wondering if you'd seen them."

Gordon yawned.

"I'll let you go to bed," I said, standing back up.

"Where are you going?" he asked as if confused by my standing.

"Actually I've got an appointment with the council."

Gordon's eyes popped open like hot corn. "You're going to meet with the Council of Seven?"

"I am."

"Boy, you've really worked yourself into something good," he whistled. "Most people would maim for that opportunity."

"Well, I'm happy to say I'll go in with no blood on my hands."

"Suit yourself," he said turning his back to me. Only moments later he began snoring. I really needed to look into the fact that Mishapians were always so tired. I would have thought longer about it, but I had a council to face.

CHAPTER NINETEEN

COUNCIL OF SEVEN

When the Harding house was first built it was by far the finest and largest home in the entire region. Flan Harding had built it with the help of his two strong sons and one brilliant daughter. Nell, his daughter, had drawn up the plans and overseen the entire project. It was said that Nell had incorporated secret rooms and passages behind the walls. Some even professed to have seen these rooms firsthand. If careful interest were taken in where the back wall sat and how deep the entry room was, one would be inclined to agree that there was more there than met the eye. Rumors of tunnels leading from under the home to a number of spots in town circulated regularly. Eyewitnesses had seen Flan Harding appear at the ward building only to be spotted at home a few minutes later. In 1970, a huge room was discovered when the Backers dug up their backyard to put in a pool. Everyone whispered that it must have been part of the secret tunnel system. In the end, however, it turned out to be Charley Tart's hidden ammo cellar.

At five minutes to ten I worked my way down the stairs and into the lobby. It was dark, but yellow light spilled in from the front porch where a single light bulb was doing its best to warm moths and give us presence. I considered flipping on an inside lamp, but the night was perfect just as it was. A few minutes later, Tat appeared dressed in a suit and wearing enough cologne to give every flower within a five-mile radius a feeling of low self-worth.

"Ready?" he asked.

"I am."

I was a little surprised when Tat simply turned and began climbing up the same stairs I had just descended.

"Did you forget something?" I questioned.

"Nope," he answered. "Just follow me."

We walked up the first two flights of stairs and then stopped at a large painted picture of a farmhouse with a couple of cows standing in front of it. I had passed by the painting hundreds of times since I had been here. Tat pulled the painting forward to reveal a door. He then took out a key, jiggled the lock, and pushed the door open. I was impressed. We stepped through the door and closed it behind us. We then crept down a walkway in a hidden space between the wall and the second floor great room.

"I had no idea all this was here," I whispered.

"There's more to this house than meets the eye," Tat said seriously. "My ancestors did some remarkable things with this place."

At the end of the passage was another door that opened without a key. We walked in and down a steep set of stairs that curled into the center of the house. At the bottom of the stairs was a huge room with a round table and seven chairs. Light came from a portable lamp that sat in the middle of the table and made everyone there look like they were about to tell a ghost story. Five of the chairs were occupied; the other two were empty. Sister Georgia Loft was there, as well as Gary Stern and his wife, Lilith the Avon lady. Next to her sat Sister Peggy Tart the librarian. Breathing down her neck was Pitt Frank. I had the distinct impression that I was seeing something that not just anyone got to view.

"Tat, he's not blindfolded," Lilith complained.

"I figured Andy didn't need it."

"But it's so much more dramatic," Gary complained.

"I have to agree," Peggy said.

"I could go out and come back in blindfolded," I offered.

"Have a seat," Pitt snapped authoritatively.

There really wasn't any place to sit besides on one of the chairs around the table. So, being proactive, I stepped over to one and pulled it towards me.

"No," Pitt stopped me. "Those are council chairs."

"So when you told me to sit you meant stand?" I asked, bringing to their attention that there was no other place to sit.

"Darnit Tat," Pitt cursed. "You were in charge of guest seating."

"Sorry," Tat apologized. "Phyllis had me doing dishes right up until ten."

"You could have called," Pitt said. It was apparent that this threatening and impressive Council of Seven still had a couple of things to get right.

"Do you mind standing?" Sister Loft asked me.

"Not at all."

"Pitt, why don't you fill Andy in on what we are and why we're here," Brother Stern asked.

Pitt huffed and then turned as if to signal by body language that he was too upset to explain.

"Tat?" Sister Loft asked.

Tat took a seat by Pitt and began to fill me in. "Many years ago when Utah was still getting into the groove of statehood, it became apparent that folks couldn't expect government to always get things right. And the Church can't force itself into local decisions about education and quality of life. So the locals here formed the Council of Seven. Seven being a rather righteous number," Tat added.

"Well, the members' identities were to be kept a secret so that bribes and egos wouldn't interfere with the decisions they made. Members serve for ten years—no longer, no shorter. At the end of their terms they simply pick someone who they feel will best fill their shoes."

Tat stopped explaining long enough to scratch and stretch. "Pending approval of the council," he continued, "that someone then steps in and replaces whoever is going out. The council makes decisions on everything from proper school plays and reading lists, to what businesses they feel belong here or how water rights are divvied up."

In summation, according to Tat, the council did a lot of good and it was a brilliant idea that the rest of the world wasn't quite ready for yet. According to me, I was a little creeped out by it all. The secret meeting place, unknown members, Tat having a position of influence?

"Why if the council is so secretive are you allowing me in to take a peek?" I asked.

"We've relaxed our standards," Tat said proudly. "In years past we would have kept you blindfolded and spoken through kazoos so as to throw you off."

Thank goodness for relaxed standards.

"So where is your seventh member?" I questioned, nodding towards the empty chair to the right of Sister Loft.

There was silence for a few seconds before Pitt Frank said, "Reinhold Hap was our seventh."

"Wow." And I meant it. The idea of Reinhold sitting on the council seemed way more progressive than I would have given any of them credit for.

"We thought it best to have the perspective of an outsider in with us," Tat explained. "Besides there really isn't anything too weird about all this. Reinhold would have claimed we were set up just to jilt him. So when Willard Cutler's term was up a while back he decided that Reinhold should be the one to step in for him."

"So what am I doing here?" I questioned, sensing that they were going to ask me to be their new seventh member. I found myself feeling incredibly flattered. Sure, there was no way that I would accept the position seeing how I couldn't commit to the ten years. But it felt good just to be considered.

"It was us that decided to get a jump on our problem and bring you in to help our struggling youth," Lilith said while looking me straight in the eyes. "Sure we needed a math teacher, but we needed more than that. Now, however, we're not sure there's hope of ever convincing anyone that there is nothing to fear in marriage," she said sadly. "Reinhold's death is like a giant black cloud hanging over us."

I tried to look compassionate and sympathetic, but I was busy wondering when the invite that I would have to turn down would come.

"So," Sister Loft took her turn. "We were wondering if you

might spend some time focusing in on who killed Reinhold instead of teaching."

"You want me to investigate?"

"Tat's been telling us what a sharp mind you have," Sister Loft said. "We figured you could focus some of your energy towards clearing up the very things that have made this place deficient in the first place. It's tearing our town apart."

Talk about requesting the impossible.

"There are law officials already working on this," I pointed out. "I can't see how I would be able to figure out anything more than they can or can't."

"They lack vision," Peggy Tart said. "You can do better."

"I don't know." I shook my head as I thought. "I don't think you would end up getting your money's worth."

"You'd be doing us a great favor," Gary insisted. "Besides, your class is broken up and we don't know what to do with you until the summer's over."

I looked at all of them as I contemplated just what to do. I had always loved mysteries. The missing plane had been on my mind ever since I had first heard of it. Besides, I already had quite a bit of information on the occurrence. Now I had been offered the opportunity to devote my summer to solving what had to be a solvable problem. Reinhold Hap was dead and the only way Mishap would ever really heal is if the truth surfaced to clear things up.

"Okay, why not," I said. "Like you said, I've got to fill the time before the school year starts anyway."

"Great!" Georgia Loft smiled. "We'll support you in any way we can. But we would prefer that no one know that we contacted you, or know who we are, or that we want you to do this."

"Thanks for the support," I joked. "What about your seventh member?" I questioned, curious as to who could possibly be a better choice than I.

"Actually, the rules state that the outgoing member must pick the next person," Lilith said. "Reinhold's death is a problem we never anticipated. You need not worry about that, however. Your job is to put Reinhold to rest."

Pitt Frank raised his hand as if commanding attention. "I want it known on the records of this council that I am completely against this outsider solving any of our mysteries."

"We know that, Pitt," Gary said sternly.

"I just don't want to have to share the blame when this all goes wrong," he snapped.

"Let's just simmer down," Tat said. "We all just want what's best for our town."

There was silence for a few moments and then Peggy spoke. "That'll be all, Andy," she said.

I was being dismissed.

"One question," Lilith asked me. "Do you mind wearing a blindfold when you leave?"

"Not at all."

Tat did the honors and then led me by the elbow back to civilization. I could tell that he was trying to be extra tricky by walking me in circles so as to throw me off so I would not be able to retrace my steps. Finally, after the twelfth time walking around the same circle I said, "Hey Tat, I'm properly confused."

"Good," he replied. He then took off my blindfold and pointed toward the door that would set me free.

"I still don't see why all this secrecy is necessary, Tat."

"Why mess with tradition?" he asked.

I didn't really wish to mess with anything at the moment.

So, I stepped out the door and into the familiar stairwell. With the painting closed I could almost pretend none of it had ever happened.

Emphasis on *almost*.

CHAPTER TWENTY

WRONG PLACE
RIGHT TIME

Thunder City had no real problems with crime until the late 1940s when Walter Melton was caught stealing chalk from the school library. Despite his confession and sincere desire to go straight, folks still recognized that their innocent little town was growing up. Things changed rapidly after that incident. There was a hit-and-run in 1962, three robberies in 1971, and senseless graffiti followed by two stolen cars in 1988. Everyone worried about what to do, but no one ever did anything besides pretend that what had just occurred was the last of the trouble.

Word of the change in my summer job description traveled pretty swiftly. It was apparent that the secret Council of Seven had some real problems with information leaks. By the time I had finished eating breakfast I had had three face-to-face and two phone conversations concerning what someone knew that they thought I should know also. After each discussion I did my best to convince them that the police might appreciate the information as well. But they always just laughed at the suggestion.

"My great-great-grandfather was a polygamist and the police tried to put him in jail," Shelly Simmons had told me over the phone. "Imagine the generations of faithful spirits that would have been snuffed out if my ancestors had gone to the police back then. They would have locked him up."

Knowing Shelly, that didn't seem like such an awful scenario.

After breakfast I noticed Phyllis peering at me through the cracked-open kitchen door. The moment our pupils locked she motioned me in. I picked up my dirty plate and carried it with me. Whatever it was she had to tell me, at least I would be accomplishing something by clearing the breakfast dishes. We were alone but her eyes darted a few times to confirm the fact.

"Andy, I know that the council has you working on the Hap case," she said, her hair appearing to turn even grayer as she spoke to me. "I don't want you doing anything that makes you feel uncomfortable."

"I won't."

"The council has a lot of weight, but they can't make you do anything if you just stand up to them."

"I appreciate that," I said kindly.

"So who exactly would you be standing up to?" she asked, making her question sound like an afterthought. "I mean, what are all the members' names?"

"Actually they've asked me not to say."

"Oh," Phyllis sounded hurt. "I guess I'll just keep fixing you meals and cleaning up after you in ignorance."

"You know I would tell you if I could."

"I can't see what it would hurt," she huffed. "Tat and his secrets. They drive me mad. Doesn't the Book of Mormon say something about secrets being bad?"

I nodded.

"Well, then I'm in the right."

"It's not that great a secret." I tried to sound comforting.

"Still," she sniffed. "Maybe it's time I started to keep a few not-so-great secrets from Tat. Starting with the fact that I played cards with Mindy Brightman last week. And we're not talking Uno.

"Anyway, I actually already know who a couple of the council members are," she informed me. "I just think it would be nice to know them all. I'm very civic-minded."

"Thank goodness for people like you," I teased.

Phyllis smiled and stared at me for a moment. She sighed and then indicated that she wanted to talk about something else by saying, "You know you sure seem to have fit in nicely here. Peggy at the library just thinks the world of you. And my daughter seems to have taken to you as well."

"Really?" I asked.

Phyllis nodded. "Sarah thinks you're just about the best teacher she's ever had. And I have to add that she, along with her mother, thinks you're one fancy piece of tinsel."

I ignored the odd compliment and sighed. "Oh, Sarah."

"Yes, Sarah. She feels really bad about class breaking up. But you've got to understand, Andy. These are dangerous times we're living in. You can't just wish a curse away."

"The curse is a farce," I said.

"I know. It's just awful."

"Summer doesn't believe in it," I said smiling to myself,

proud that I had found a way to bring Phyllis's other daughter into the conversation.

"Summer has always been my challenge," Phyllis said while massaging her own hair. "She does what she wants and does it so well that I can't complain."

"That's not a bad deal," I pointed out.

"I suppose," Phyllis frowned. "But even Summer hasn't found love."

" . . . yet," I added for her.

"Something needs to happen to this town," she said, ignoring my *yet*. "It's as if none of us really know each other. That's why Tat had such hope in you, Andy. He figured that if we could get our young people in a room together for a few days a week that they might begin to fall for one another."

"Sorry it didn't work out," I said.

"It just stinks." She sighed. "Well, I've got rolls rising. If you change your mind and decide to start sharing secrets let me know."

"You'll be the first person I spill to."

Phyllis walked off and left me alone.

"It just stinks," I said to myself. She was right. I felt enough for Mishap to feel that I had failed. I wanted this town to be comfortable in its own skin. I wanted the air to be less negatively charged when it came to the prospects of marriage. "It just stinks," I said again. For some reason the words reminded me of the odd pews the ward had.

An idea popped into my head.

Perhaps there was a contribution I could make after all.

CHAPTER TWENTY-ONE

WHEN THE SAINTS COME BARGING IN

I waited until Gordon was sound asleep and the clock said 1:00. Then I climbed out of bed and crept quietly down the stairs. I opened the front door as silently as I could and slipped out. The night was warm and dark with no hint of changing who it was. I sneaked into the garage that Tat had converted into a workshop and retrieved the item my mischief required. I then walked along the edge of the road sticking to the blackest night for the sake of not being seen.

I was on a mission.

I reached the chapel and crept around the back, over to the far door. It suddenly occurred to me that I really had not thought out what I was going to do. I fiddled with one of the windows hoping it was open. It wasn't. I messed with the side door trying to see if there was some way of getting in without doing any damage to the building. Everything seemed secured. I was just about to call myself a fool for the tenth time and walk back home when I discovered that the front door was unlocked.

It had to be an indication that God was with me.

I opened the door quietly and slipped inside. I headed straight for the chapel, stopping only once to get a drink at the drinking fountain. I wasn't really thirsty, but I don't think I have it in me to pass a water fountain without trying it out.

As I was wiping my mouth I heard a low moan. I thought at first that it was an indication that God was now miffed at me. But the moaning seemed near and earthly. I listened with feeling. There was someone in the chapel. I couldn't believe it. Here it was one o'clock in the morning and someone had the nerve to interfere with my interfering by being here. I considered packing it in and heading out, but it occurred to me that someone moaning in a chapel at one in the morning just might need help.

I walked to the wide doors and pressed slowly against them. It was too dark to know instantly who was inside so I stepped through and whispered. "Hello?"

The moaning stopped.

"Who's there?" I asked, wondering whether or not I should flick on the lights.

"It's just me," a voice answered back. "The bishop."

I decided to leave the lights off seeing how the two of us still had not had a face-to-face concerning the misinformation he had received about his wife and me.

"Andy, is that you?"

"Yes."

"What are you doing here?" he asked.

"I was wondering the same thing about you."

My eyes were beginning to adjust to the dark. A small amount of night light drifted in through the tiny windows that ran along the top of the chapel walls. I walked to the front of the chapel and found him sitting on the first row. I started to partially explain myself. "I was just out taking a walk and noticed the door was unlocked," I lied.

"Do you usually take late night walks with a saw?" he questioned, nodding towards the saw I had pulled out of Tat's garage and was now carrying.

"It's a dangerous world we live in," I tried to joke.

He only sighed.

"Are you all right, Bishop?"

"Actually it's sort of fitting that you would find me here," he admitted. "I've been thinking about you and my Maggie."

"There's nothing to us," I said. "You know that, don't you?"

"I do," he breathed. "She told me this evening about you and the tree and the kiss."

"And the fact that it took place over ten years ago," I added.

He nodded. And then for some reason he just started to talk. "You know I thought when I was put in as bishop that everything would just fall into place. I grew up in this ward and always figured that with the right leadership we could be a much closer group of people. I've done nothing to make us that way," he lamented. "And my job. It just keeps pulling me further and further away from any sort of stability. It took Maggie talking about that kiss to point out how much work my own marriage and family needs. My kids didn't even know that I like to play 'Cheater,'" he moaned.

He had lost me with that one. "Is that pretty bad?" I asked compassionately.

"Cheater was my favorite board game when I was a kid," he cried. "I used to love to play it with my dad. I would always land on his piece and send him back to his home space yelling, 'Cheaters never prosper.' He always let me win and I never got tired of him letting me."

The bishop sniffed.

"Tonight my kids got out Cheater and started playing it. When I saw what they were doing I told them that I loved that game and asked if I could join them. You should have seen their faces, Andy. It was as if I had just told them that they needed to go out and get jobs to support their mother and me. They were in complete shock. They couldn't believe that their dad liked the same game they did. They didn't even know I knew about games. What kind of father keeps those kind of things from his children?"

"A busy one," I answered, not sure if he was actually expecting an answer.

"I want to be a better dad."

"It's not too late," I tried. "Maggie loves you and your kids are young."

Bishop Hearth sat up straight. "I'm just no good at changing."

"Neither am I," I said. "Yet here I am living in some Utah town trying to justify my being here by solving a mystery."

He looked at me and tried to smile. I sat down next to him, putting the saw on the ground.

"I don't know if I really can change," the bishop lamented.

"I think you do," I said gently.

"But—"

"Now."

"Maggie really is a great wife," he conceded. "I couldn't live with myself if I thought I was making her miserable."

"Well then make her happy," I said, having no real wisdom or honest psychology on the matter.

"It is possible," he tried to convince himself.

"I can't imagine how I could help," I said. "But if you guys want me to watch your kids so that you can get away for a few days I'd be happy to."

"Really? My kids?" he said with genuine surprise.

"Sure. They could teach me how to play Cheaters."

"You're a nice guy, Andy."

"How about giving me a calling then?"

Bishop Hearth just smiled. "I came here tonight because I couldn't think of another place to go," he said. "It must have been inspiration. Thanks, Andy."

"I didn't do anything."

He gained his composure and glanced once again at my saw. "So what's the real story behind that?" he asked.

"Bishop," I said. "I have a confession to make."

I explained to him about my wicked desire to come here and saw off the backs of all the high-rising pews. I told him about feeling bad about my class falling through and how I felt that it might make a difference if the ward members could actually see each other on Sunday.

"I had never really thought about it," he admitted. "We've always been so proud of our handcarved pews."

"Sorry," I apologized. "I don't know what I was thinking."

"I'm happy that you saw the error of your ways," he smiled.

I stood and picked up my saw.

"Thanks, Andy," he said again. "I mean it."

"Thank you," I said. "You've saved me from a life of crime."

As I was walking out he stopped me by asking, "Any chance of me borrowing that saw for a couple of days?"

"Sure," I shrugged. "It's Tat's after all."

"I've been working on my home office and this could really come in handy."

"It's all yours," I said, handing it over.

"Good night, Andy."

"Good night, Bishop."

I walked home in relative quiet. I say relative because for some reason I thought I could hear the extremely faint sound of a power saw running.

CHAPTER TWENTY-TWO

BLAME IT ON THE PRICE OF GAS

Thunder City had once been considerably harder to get to. When Cornelious Thunder had first arrived, there was no road leading anywhere near it. One of the first projects the Saints took on was mapping out where the best route into town would be. Some argued that folks should approach their city from the east so as to get the best view of the Wayne River. Others insisted that a path coming in from the west would show off the open prairies and the small bump of Lop Rock. As a compromise, the town built switchbacks that headed both east and west many times over. After some growth, the state of Utah paved the lower switchbacks and straightened out the winding road that led up to them. Seven years previously, the two-lane highway was widened and a center lane was put in so that people could pass and turn with greater safety. Since that time, accidents had increased thirty-five percent.

I honestly don't know why I did it. Honest. It just seemed like a smart thing to do at the time. I needed to get to Salt Lake City and Summer was heading that direction. My car still didn't work and Summer had a well-running vehicle. Gas prices were high and the prophet had told us repeatedly to be frugal and spendthrifty. I enjoyed Summer's company and a nice road trip with her would be very enjoyable.

Four fine reasons.

Sure one could be trivial and petty by bringing up the fact that I was going to Salt Lake City to see Lauren. That same small-minded person could also argue that mixing Lauren and Summer in any way was both complicated and cruel. But to those who would bring up those facts, I say, "shame on you." Can't a man do unto himself, as he would have others do unto him?

"I like this drive," Summer said as we pulled away from Mishap and picked up speed.

I looked at her and agreed wholeheartedly. She smiled at me as if she were only just now realizing what she was in for by spending her morning traveling with me.

"I think I'm in love," I said casually as we crested a plain and stared into the open drive ahead of us.

"Really?"

"Utah is one beautiful place."

"Whew," Summer sighed.

"A person can love more than one thing at a time," I added. "Just because I'm infatuated with the landscape doesn't mean I can't invest my heart in other options."

"Are you trying to sound clever?"

I shook my head, stopped, and then reluctantly said, "Yes."

"So you're meeting an old friend at the airport?" Summer asked.

"Yep."

"Thanks for going into such detail."

"There's not much to say," I said. "An old friend is flying through, and I thought it might be nice to visit them on their stop."

"How charitable."

"I pride myself on giving until it hurts."

"Hurts who?"

I watched Summer's blue eyes follow a small purple car that passed us and then sped off. I could tell that even though her vision followed one path her thoughts were speeding down another.

"Hey, Andy." She turned towards me. "Do you think there is something wrong with Thunder City?"

"Wrong like bad?"

"Just wrong."

"Well, someone was killed. And there is that missing plane thing. And the curse. Oh, and there's that secretive Council of Seven that seems to enjoy making decisions for others. And people seem to be constantly falling asleep. Hmm . . . Nope."

"Not that kind of wrong," Summer said. She smiled, her dark hair falling nicely on her shoulders as she drove. "I don't know. It sounds dumb, but I was reading the journal I kept at college and it reads like someone besides me wrote it. If you compared my journal entry from yesterday to mine back at school it seems like they were written by two different people."

"You've grown into a fine young woman."

"Seriously, Andy."

"All right, then, don't you think it's possible you could have changed some?"

"*Some* sure. But . . . I guess I'm just being silly."

"Sorry, Summer," I said sincerely. "I'm just not sure what you're getting at."

She breathed evenly for a few moments. "Sometimes I worry about Mishap making me stupid. It just seems different since I've returned."

"It is a small town," I pointed out. "There's not much to make a person feel cultured and progressive."

"We've got culture," she defended.

"Do you mean the horseshoe tournaments they hold every Tuesday night at the city park?"

"I mean our town has a history."

"So do most of the world's most debilitating diseases," I pointed out.

"This is going to be a long ride."

"Listen," I said. "If it makes you feel any better I've been in Mishap for a short while now and I don't feel any less smart then I did before."

"That helps," she joked.

We both stared at the horizon for a few miles. I let the hum of her truck move me slowly closer to her. Before long I was leaning so near she couldn't ignore me.

"What are you doing?" she asked.

"I just wanted to see if you had a better view than I did."

Surprisingly she seemed to be more charmed than annoyed.

"I like you, Summer," I said sincerely, moved by the fact that she had such tremendous patience for me.

"There's no accounting for taste," she replied.

"Let's elope," I joked. "Let's just keep on driving until we reach Las Vegas. We could be married by sunrise."

"How enticing."

"I'll even let you hyphenate your last name."

Summer looked deeply at me for a brief moment. She spoke with her eyes. I didn't know she was capable of such language. I would have leaned in and kissed her if it had not been for the fact that we were flying forward at about seventy miles an hour on a three-lane highway.

"So tell me about this old friend of yours that you're meeting," Summer said, wisely changing the topic at hand.

"Not much to tell," I said.

"Do they have a name?"

"Big L," I answered, still not wanting to let her know too much about Lauren.

"He or a she?"

"Ummm . . . she," I said slowly.

"Not easy to tell?"

"It's just never mattered."

"Really?"

"I only see the inside of people."

"You're so accepting."

"Does that mean you'll marry me?" I asked.

"Why not?" Summer shrugged.

"I'll hold you to that."

We tried to get into a conversation about movies but that went nowhere. Summer brought up books, but we couldn't seem to make that discussion entertaining. So, we traveled in silence for a while until we came up behind a slow moving van. Summer stayed back a comfortable distance looking for just the right moment to pass.

"Now," I challenged.

"No way," she said, not able to see far enough ahead of her to deem the pass safe.

"Now," I said a few moments later.

"Andy."

"Just trying to help."

I would have gone on desperately trying to be entertaining, but the van in front of us suddenly swerved. It pulled so quickly to the right that Summer didn't have time to see the huge deer that it had been swerving to miss. The truck slammed into the back end of the deer throwing the poor animal into the brush alongside the road. Summer braked as if she had just spotted a hitchhiking leprechaun sitting on a pot of gold. The truck tires dug loudly into the earth on the road's shoulder. The van that had caused this kept on flying down the road.

"Are you okay?" I asked after we had jerked to a stop.

"Fine," Summer said. She jumped quickly from her truck. I figured she was getting out to see what damage had been done to the front corner of her vehicle. I unbuckled and leaped out of my side and up to the front of the truck. Though there was some damage, there was no Summer. I spotted her a hundred feet back looking at the wounded animal. I ran as quickly to her as I could, hoping that she hadn't seen me giving more com-passion to the truck than the deer.

I stopped and stared at the struggling animal as he lay on the ground. Summer had her hands on her knees and was look-ing closely at the damage.

"Is he okay?"

"I don't think so," she said.

"Do you want me to shoot him?" I asked, sincerely wanting to help.

She ignored my comment by asking me to help her get the deer into the back of her truck.

I would have much rather shot him.

Summer made me take the end that was causing the animal so much pain at the moment. As we shifted him, warm blood began to soak my arm. I tried to, "eewww" in as manly a way as possible. Summer pushed as I pulled. I don't know if it was the warmth, or the smell, or just the fact that I was trying to show that I was man enough to lift a two-hundred-and-fifty-pound deer without effort. Whatever the reason I was suddenly fading. I could actually feel the blood drop from my head to my feet.

"Are you okay, Andy?" Summer asked as we shuffled.

"I . . ."

I never finished my sentence. The next thing I knew I was coming to in Summer's arms. She had my head in her lap and was trying to revive me. I could hear and feel cars flying by us. I opened my eyes slowly and looked at her as she tried not to smile.

"This looks bad doesn't it?" I said in embarrassment.

"Don't worry about it, buddy," I heard an unknown voice behind us say. I sat up—much too quickly—to see a huge man in a flannel ball cap staring at me. He was doing nothing to hold back his smile.

"This gentleman saw me kneeling over you when I was try-ing to revive you," Summer explained. "He stopped to see if he could help."

If there had been an airport anywhere within a ten-mile radius I would have jumped up, ran there, and bought myself a ticket to anyplace besides here.

"Seriously," Mr. Big tried to sound comforting. "Don't be

ashamed. I've got a young daughter that gets white as a sheet every time she sees one of our stock giving birth."

Ashamed was far too mild a word.

I looked over at the deer.

"He didn't make it," Summer informed me.

How I envied that animal.

Summer and her new friend tried to help me to my feet.

"I'm fine," I said, trying to wave them away.

A monstrous semi flew past us causing us all to sway and making me look less steady than I actually was.

"If you'd like I could follow you guys for a while to see if he's all right," the man whispered to Summer.

"I think we'll be fine," she whispered back. "Thanks for your help."

"I'll get animal control to pick up the deer," were his parting words as he walked off and climbed into his truck.

I got into Summer's vehicle and tried to think of some way to explain what had happened to me. A number of excuses flashed through my mind but all of them made me look just as pathetic as the truth. Summer got in and put her keys into the ignition. I thought it best to explain myself before we proceeded.

"I'm . . . "

Summer began laughing so hard that I began to fear for the smooth rotation of the earth. When she came up for air the fourth time I tried to defend myself.

"I don't know why . . . "

She had some manners to work on. I'm fairly certain that most cultures in the world consider violently laughing at someone who was uncomfortable as rude. When she finished a few minutes later I asked, "Finished?"

"Almost," she laughed.

"I usually don't faint on the first drive," I said with embarrassment.

"Don't worry, I like sensitive men," she continued laughing.

"Really." I almost begged, "You have to understand. I have no idea what happened. I've seen thousands of operations on the medical cable channel and never even flinched."

"It's okay, Andy."

"Right," I sighed. I mimicked her, "'Don't worry Andy. Just know that every time I look at you from now on I'll think about you dropping off on the side of the highway.'"

"Not every time," she said with a smile.

I had never been the kind of guy that felt he had to fit perfectly into the male stereotype. I was content with who I was and secure in my gender. At the moment, however, I felt as if I needed to prove to her that I was fit to be male. I said a few lame things and she followed up with, "Really, Andy. I don't think less of you. It's a warm day—that's all."

I decided then and there to simply shut up and never speak again. She decided then and there only to burst into laughter three more times before we reached Salt Lake City.

I think I was being the bigger person.

CHAPTER TWENTY-THREE

CUTTING MY LOSSES

Summer dropped me off at the airport and promised that she would pick me up at the arranged spot on Monday morning so that we could drive back to Mishap together. I changed into a blood-free shirt in the airport bathroom and then walked to the gate where the screen promised Lauren's flight would be arriving.

Her plane came in five minutes early.

Lauren was the first person off the plane. She hugged me and then said that Salt Lake City smelled funny. We took a shuttle to downtown Salt Lake and spent the evening walking around Temple Square and eating dinner on the top floor of the Joseph Smith Memorial Building.

"I could be Mormon," she said as she poked pasta with her silver fork.

"You could?" I questioned.

"I mean, it's not like you guys sacrifice things or make the women wear shawls over their heads."

I told her about how some Saints had practiced polygamy in the early days.

We went to our separate hotel rooms around midnight and then reconnected at around ten the next morning. We attended sacrament meeting at the Joseph Smith building, had some lunch, and then wasted the rest of the afternoon walking the streets and stopping anywhere that looked remotely historic or interesting. As darkness fell we sat near the Conference Center and watched people walk around.

"Everyone looks happy," Lauren commented.

"They're paid actors," I joked.

"I've decided to stay a few days longer," she announced. "Maybe I'll go back to your town with you."

"You have?" I asked, suddenly feeling panicked.

"We need more time together."

"Lauren, we need to come to terms with the fact that the two of us are just too different for our relationship to work, or for us to want the same future."

"I might surprise you," she smiled coyly.

"You already have," I said, referring to her announcement to stay.

"Your friend won't mind if I drive back with you two will he?"

What could I say but, "Yes?"

"Come on, Andy," she laughed. "I want to see where you're living."

"Lauren," I protested.

"You mean to say that you don't care enough to do this for me?" She pouted.

"It's not that."

"Then what is it?"

Thoughts of Summer filled me like sunlight on a white beach. How could I begin to tell Lauren what I really felt? I had tried not to lead her on, but she had pushed my reasoning aside and shown up here anyway. Now I was put in the position of having to show my past to what I wanted to be my future. Sure, Summer might never look at me in an attractive light again after the deer incident. But, seriously, I didn't want to count her out just yet. And as much as I didn't want to count Summer out I didn't want to count Lauren in.

"Lauren."

"Andy."

"I just think it would be best to let this year pass and then see how we feel." I was trying to let her down easy.

"Fine," she huffed. "If you can't take three days out of your life to please me then I'll just be on my way."

"I don't want to hurt you," I reasoned. "Honest."

"Too late," she said. Tears were welling up in her eyes.

I felt awful. I didn't want to hurt Lauren, but I couldn't see what good would come from stringing things along. She was beautiful, intelligent, and fun to be with, but our relationship had never seemed to move beyond that. Even if Lauren joined the Church and suddenly magically desired the same things that I wanted out of life, it still wouldn't be right. She just wasn't the one. I needed to be honest. "I suppose it wouldn't hurt for you to come visit a few days," I heard myself say.

I was such a coward. If Summer didn't think I was a wimp because of the deer incident, she'd still eventually find out I truly had no backbone.

"Do you mean it, Andy?"

I nodded weakly.

"I know we may not be perfect, but I want to see if there's anything left to us."

"I just don't want to make this a bigger mess than it needs to be."

"It'll be great," she said. "You'll see."

I didn't believe a word she was saying.

CHAPTER TWENTY-FOUR

THREE CHEERS

I must admit that I was pleasantly surprised by the fact that Summer appeared guardedly jealous when she met Lauren. She recovered quickly though, talking about how fun it would be to have a third person driving back with us. Lauren didn't take to Summer with such ease. I could see that she was extremely bothered by the fact that the friend I was traveling with was not only *not* a he, but was a spectacularly pretty she. Lauren bit her lip and tried to look as if it didn't bother her, but she wasn't all that convincing. Halfway home Summer decided to tell Lauren the deer story.

"*Fainted?*" Lauren asked, sounding as if she didn't know men were capable of actually doing that.

"It was warm," I said lamely.

"That's true," Summer said. "I think it was a scorching seventy-eight degrees at the moment of Andy's collapse."

Lauren looked as if she were embarrassed.

When we pulled into Mishap we went directly to the Harding house. Tat was on the front porch folding origami frogs out of old, unclaimed letters. He welcomed Lauren and then invited her to stay right with us at the Harding house for the whole of her time here. I secretly cursed Tat's gracious nature. He took her bags and walked her in to find an empty room. This left me standing alone on the porch with Summer.

"I like her, Andy," Summer said in reference to Lauren.

"I *like* her too," I said. "We used to date and now she just can't seem to let us end."

"Oh."

"Listen, Summer," I said seriously, looking into her deep blue eyes. "I know this was kind of a weird trip, but I was really hoping that there might be more to you and me."

"More what?" Summer asked.

"More everything," I said. "I just don't want Lauren to ruin what could be something good."

"I won't let her if you don't." Summer smiled.

I really liked Summer Harding.

Lauren came back out onto the porch and asked us both what we were talking about.

"Nothing," we said in unison.

It was the most suspicious answer we could have given. Fortunately Gordon walked up to the house and stopped to admire Lauren. He told us all how he had just been down at Roy's taxidermy shop helping Roy gut his latest project.

"Gut?" Lauren asked.

"Clean it out," he explained coolly.

"Doesn't that make you sick?" Lauren questioned, eyeing him as if a single glance couldn't tell her everything. She was obviously curious as to whether all men were squeamish when it came to blood and guts.

"Nah," Gordon blushed. "I'm real used to messy situations."

I could have been wrong, but I think Lauren batted her

eyelashes at him. A sort of light settled on her and she looked like the girl I had met in the library all that while ago.

"You remind me of someone," Lauren informed Gordon. "Have you read any of Gonzala Heratio's poetry?"

"Is he from Utah?" Gordon asked innocently.

Lauren laughed as if he were the funniest person she had ever met.

"What do you do, Gordon?" she asked.

"I have my own business. Would you like to see it?" he asked shyly.

"Sure," Lauren said. I could tell that even she was unsure of what she was doing. "I'll be right back, Andy," she informed me while looking at Gordon.

"Take your time," I insisted.

Gordon nodded towards the store and Lauren followed. Once again Summer and I were alone.

"What was that?" I asked in confusion.

"I have no idea," Summer confessed. "It almost looked like they were flirting."

Tat came out and asked us both if we would help him race his hopping paper frogs.

"When I compete against myself I always win," he lamented.

The three of us raced frogs across the porch until Bert and Annie Lawson strolled by and started complaining about how they never did anything fun anymore. Tat invited them to join us, and they jumped at the opportunity. As I poked at my folded piece of paper I thought to myself how much Mishap was soaking into me. The sky dimmed a bit, and Phyllis brought us lemonade and informed us that dinner would be ready in ten minutes.

When we all went inside, Bert and Annie took the two spots

that Gordon and Lauren would have taken at the dinner table. I suggested the name, "Ned," for their unborn child.

Bert passed me the mashed potatoes. "Dead Ned?" Bert said, as if disgusted by my lack of compassion. "You know he would be teased mercilessly. Dead Ned wet the bed."

I dropped the conversation.

Actually, there was really big news at the dinner table. That Sunday when the town had gone to church they were all surprised to discover that their pews had been trimmed down.

"Oddest thing," Tat said bewildered. "No one knows who did it."

"I kind of liked it," Annie said. "I had no idea just how many people we have in our ward."

"Me too," Phyllis said. "It was so nice to stare at the back of the Tart family instead of just looking at wood."

"I don't know," Tat said. "Jonathan Skew put his heart and soul in to those seats."

"I'm sure Jonathan could care less what we do with them," Summer insisted. "I can't believe someone didn't cut those things down years ago. Whoever thought of doing that was inspired."

I had never been so secretly proud of myself before. I was also quite impressed with Bishop Hearth's ability to carry out a good idea.

After dinner we all played a few hands of Uno and then tried one unsuccessful round of charades. The party broke up around ten and we all drifted off our separate ways. I went to bed before Gordon had returned from his evening with Lauren. I would have worried about subjecting Lauren to the personality of Gordon, but she had gone on her own recognizance. I was curious as to whether or not Gordon really did look like Gonzala Heratio. If he honestly did, I suddenly didn't feel so bad about never stacking up to the poet.

It was nice to fall asleep without the sound of Gordon snoring.

CHAPTER TWENTY-FIVE

THINGS WERE GETTING HARRIET

Lop Rock was so named because the word *lop* sounded good with the word *rock*. The explanation got no more complicated than that. At the moment, it sat beautifully next to Knock Pond. But when Cornelious and his band of Saints had first wandered into the area the rock sat alone. It was sticking up like a broken bone that had pushed through the earth's skin. A number of weird symbols had been carved into the base of the rock.

When the writing was first noticed, Dever Scotch claimed that they were the markings of a great Nephite warrior who had passed that way many years ago. His tale was taken as gospel until a few years later when some foreign immigrants passed though and pointed out that the letters were actually Chinese characters. A smarter man than Dever might have taken this as his cue to back off, but Dever pushed forward. He told everyone that this simply supported the fact that the Nephites really did come from China like the Book of Mormon said. When someone asked Dever if he had actually ever read the Book of

Mormon he started to cry and bore his testimony about adversity and the sweet fruit that often came from it.

It turned out that Gordon and Lauren had spent the evening at the Thunder City park staring at the stars and wondering where each other had been all their lives. According to Gordon, Lauren had gone on and on about how she thought she once loved me. But then she told him that I wouldn't really work for her seeing that I was so fickle and uncommitted. Besides, there was something about Gordon that had hit her at first sight. After the two of them established that I wasn't in the picture any longer, they simply lay under the stars as Lauren told Gordon about all the things he had never realized he wanted to know. She told him about life back east and about education and wars and tragedy and laws and life. And Gordon listened.

I was amazed. Gordon was turning into a human being. I think the appearance of Lauren had shocked him into wanting to know more. I couldn't have been more pleased.

I spent all day Tuesday at the public library looking up anything and everything that I felt could be connected to the mystery of Mishap and the death of Reinhold. I got a lot of information from newspapers and books, but the greatest source was the thousands of journals the library had. Mishap was truly a town full of journal-keeping people. There were copies and actual journals from just about everyone that had ever lived here. I was impressed and amazed. I spent hour after hour reading up on every facet and personality that Thunder City had. My brain was still insisting that I could figure this all out if only I had the right information. So, I kept at it until dinnertime. I then returned to the Harding house and engaged in some heated games of Ping-Pong with Tat. Right after my first loss, a huge storm began rolling into town. Clouds crammed the sky with their cotton bodies and wet souls. And just as I was about to secure my first win, Summer came by to inform me that Mrs. Hap had just been spotted on the lake.

"You're kidding?" I asked with excitement.

"Randall Crammer was out there with the young men of the ward and there she was—larger than life."

I didn't need further prompting. I dropped my paddle and took Summer's hand. I had been waiting impatiently for the chance to finally come face-to-face with Harriet Hap. It looked like the waiting was over.

Gordon and Lauren were sitting out on the porch and talking about politics and the possible war that was brewing in the Middle East. We offered them a chance to come with us and they took it. We all hopped into Summer's truck and took off towards Knock Pond. Rain began to fall lightly, as the storm grew stronger.

"You think she'll still be there?" I asked.

"If the clouds break up enough to let the moon shine through," Gordon said smartly.

When we reached the pond the wind was howling and there were a few other cars parked, their occupants hoping to witness the mystery in action. It was nice to have company seeing how the dark night and choppy water made the environment rather eerie.

"We need to get up on top of Lop Rock," Gordon said. "You can't see much from down here."

I took Summer's hand as Gordon took Lauren's, and we

stomped through the wet brush and over to the base of Lop Rock. The air was wet but no real rain was falling now. Wind continued to blow, making the pond restless and wild. Clouds were strewn across the dark sky like thick fluffy blemishes. The full moon darted quickly between them.

The short trail to the top of Lop Rock was wet and steep. I helped pull Summer up and then gave assistance to Lauren as she gave Gordon a boost. I don't think I had ever been more excited. Just as we got to the edge of Lop Rock the clouds covered the moon completely, making the lake look pitch black.

"They'll move out in a moment," Summer said putting her arm around my side.

All four of us stood there in the blowing wind, waiting for heaven to shed a little light on the situation. I looked at Lauren as she held Gordon's hand. She caught me staring and smiled.

"I'm glad you came," I said honestly.

"Me too," she laughed, looking as if she were amazed by her own words. "I hope you're not upset about how it all turned out. I don't know what it is about this place, but I suddenly feel awake."

"It is a bit different here than . . . "

I would have gone on, but the clouds broke and heavy light smeared like neon frosting across the choppy water. I don't know what I was expecting, but what I saw was far from anything I had imagined. I guess I had thought that the image would be some sort of faded shading that—if you squinted—looked like a distorted face. But now as I gazed down at the tumultuous water, a huge female face stared straight at us.

All four of us took a step back.

"I can't believe it," Lauren whispered above the winds.

"She wasn't a pretty woman," Gordon explained.

They had both taken the words right from my mouth. The waves stirred and the face upon the water seemed to mouth the word *marriage* over and over. I could honestly see how people had thought the town was cursed. Heck, I was tempted to push Summer away from me before the pond spotted the two of us together.

"She's brighter than ever," Gordon said in amazement.

"I haven't seen her for months," Summer said above the wind. "I don't remember it being so big."

I wanted desperately to rationally explain what I was seeing, but as I glanced around I couldn't see anything worldly that could have been producing what I now saw.

"That gives me the creeps," I heard a couple of people standing next to us say to one another.

"It really is an uneasy feeling," Summer said.

Lauren let Gordon hold her tight. I contemplated how to make sense of what I saw. The light from the moon angling in against the stormy water did not explain the phenomenon. I contemplated the clouds and the reflection the image made as it bounced off their undersides.

"Let's get out of here," Summer suggested.

"I'm game," Gordon said. "I'd like to be as far away from this as possible."

I could tell that Gordon was having a hard time feeling good about Lauren with a gigantic woman cursing marriage down below him.

"How is it possible?" I questioned. The wind had picked up and I was not quite yet willing to go.

"It's a miracle," Gordon explained.

"Miracles have a purpose," I said. "This is no miracle."

"Who cares," Gordon complained. "Maybe it's one of those

bad miracles. Which means that we should get the heck out of here."

"Come on, Andy." Summer pulled on my arm.

Let me just say that there really are few things I find more persuasive than Summer tugging me in her direction. But for some reason I couldn't stop staring at Harriet Hap.

"Come on," Summer said again.

I started to turn with her and then stopped. The moon surged through a huge break in the blowing clouds. I dropped Summer's hand and stepped closer to the edge.

"Andy, what are you doing?" Gordon asked.

I don't know what it was inside of me that was making me feel the way I did. Maybe it was my need to show Summer that I was braver than a fainting Good Samaritan. Or perhaps the part of me that used to jump out of trees after I had kissed a girl was resurfacing. Captain Matrimony was not dead. Whatever it was, I turned from all of them and ran the two steps to the edge of Lop Rock. Then with a gigantic leap I threw myself over the edge and down into the face of Harriet Hap. The image raced towards me like a thundering light. I could hear the screams of those I left behind as the water pulled up around me and I fell deep beneath.

CHAPTER TWENTY-SIX

LOOK OUT BELOW

The water blurred my sight, making things underwater look bigger than they probably were. I was surprised to see how light it was below the waves. I would have pondered this point a little bit longer, but as I shot back up to the surface a huge dark object came hurling at me from above. Gordon landed right on top of me, hitting my right shoulder and sending me back down to the bottom of the pond. My feet touched and I pushed up as hard as I could. When I broke the surface I could hear Gordon yelling my name.

"Andy! Andy!"

"I'm right here!" I hollered.

Gordon swam the few strokes between us and wrapped his arm tightly around my neck. I tried to yell but his arm was cutting off my air intake. He dragged me backward to the shore. The waves of the lake were splashing like mad as the wind continued to stir up the water.

"Gordon!" I finally got out.

"Hang on, I've got you!"

That was just what I didn't want. He pulled me up onto land and then rolled over to catch his breath. I sat up just as Summer and Lauren reached the bottom of Lop Rock. They ran directly towards Gordon and me.

"What were you doing?" Summer hollered at me, sounding as if she didn't know whether she should be embarrassed or compassionate.

"I don't know. I guess I just wanted to see what was down there," I explained as I rubbed my shoulder where Gordon had hit me.

The wind howled fiercely as others in the area approached us and asked if I was all right.

"In a sense," Summer answered.

Gordon and I picked ourselves up. My right foot throbbed madly. Summer noticed my pain.

"What's the matter?"

"I must have hurt my foot when Gordon pushed me back down to the bottom of the pond."

"I can't believe you jumped in," Summer said.

"I couldn't help it."

It was an excuse I had used often in life. I seemed to do far too many things that I wouldn't ever have done had I been myself. I could remember once in third grade during one of our blessed activity afternoons, my teacher, Miss Jenkins, had given us all permission to roam around the room freely—to read books or draw on the chalkboard. Jeff Shaw and I decided that the best way to spend our time was playing a game of hangman on the front board. I went first, taking my time to come up with a well-thought-out word and then drawing what I still to this day feel was a rather authentic looking hangman's gallows. The first letter Jeff guessed was wrong. I wrote the letter to the side of the gallows near the top of the board, drew a head on the rope, and went on. Jeff's next guess got him no closer to the solution. I wrote down his second failed attempt. The third letter was a no go. I marked down his missed character with flare. I was so caught up in my desire to win that I hadn't caught on to the fact that Jeff was picking his letters carefully— letters that if lined up next to each other spelled a word I wasn't comfortable *hearing,* much less *writing* in front of my whole third grade class. As I wrote down the fourth missed letter and completed the word, Petra Shoe spotted my deed and yelled to Miss Jenkins. I had caught on too late. I stared at the word I had just written dumbfounded. My parents were called, I was grounded for a good chunk of my adolescence, and Jeff Shaw didn't receive an invitation to my next birthday party.

"So are you going to be okay?" Summer asked me as we walked away from the pond.

"I hope so."

We got back to the truck and Summer drove us home. Gordon and Lauren split off once we got there. Apparently Lauren wanted to talk to him about how brave he had been by diving in after me. I wished Summer felt the same way about her boyfriend's heroics, but I think she was more worried than impressed. She took me upstairs and tucked me in bed, insisting that I needed some rest.

She got no argument from me.

CHAPTER TWENTY-SEVEN

MOB RULES

I n the spring of 1952 Florence Loft lost track of her daughter Georgia while hanging clothes on her line to dry. She had been thinking of other things while pinning and whistling. When Florence finally turned her attention to her child, the girl was gone. Thunder City came out to help. Town members combed groves and fields while anybody with a phone or feet did their best to spread the word.

By late afternoon Georgia was still missing. A misdirected local suggested that perhaps she might have been snatched up by Fred Cord, the town pharmacist. After all, Fred had a problem with taking things that weren't his. Sure he had never actually harmed or kidnapped anyone, but he had kept Homer Davis's bowling ball and pretended like it was his. He had also mysteriously ended up with Gomer Upshaw's spare car battery. These things, in light of Georgia's disappearance, seemed to shine the light of suspicion on him with blinding force. So the town banded together and trudged over to Fred's home. They stormed the place accusing Fred of things he had been no part of. Shortly after the town took justice into their own hands,

Meyer Loft, Florence's husband and Georgia's father, appeared carrying Georgia in his arms and wondering what everyone was fussing about. Apparently while Florence had been pinning and whistling Meyer had told her that he was taking Georgia to Salt Lake City and that he would be back later in the day. Fred Cord let the accusation slide and returned the bowling ball to Homer. Many years later Georgia was called to serve as Relief Society president of the Thunder City First Ward.

I don't know if it was the loud sound of rain against the roof or all the noise that Gordon made when he came in and went to bed that woke me up. Either way, I was up and the dark, rainy night seemed to make my mind jump all over. There was something about the dream that I had been having that made me overly confused. There had been gravel and rocks and some sort of construction site. Pitt Frank had been there as well as Tat. My mind shivered and clicked like a loose gate on a windy day. I lay still for a few more minutes when suddenly inspiration dropped from above and blew me to my feet, even though my right one still throbbed from my experience in the pond.

"That's it," I practically screamed.

Gordon woke, wrestled with his blanket, and then fell to the floor. "Andy, what are you doing?" he asked as I was putting on my shoes.

"I know where the plane is," I said excitedly.

"You do?"

"I do!"

I grabbed my shirt and ran down the stairs and over to Tat's room. I knocked on the door and waited. Eventually Tat cracked open the door and squinted at me like I was made in the image of something he would never understand.

"Andy, it's almost midnight."

"I know where the plane is," I insisted.

"What? How could you?"

"I'll show you."

Tat was much faster than Gordon at throwing his clothes on, though in fairness to Gordon at least he matched. Tat on the other hand looked to be wearing a mishmash of clothing articles, two of which appeared to be Phyllis's. We walked out into the rain and jumped into the mail truck. Tat pulled a light from the glove box and placed it on top of the vehicle. A polite siren rang weakly through the air.

"Where to?" Tat asked.

"Pitt's place."

"Andy?" Tat said with concern.

"Trust me, Tat."

He pulled out of the drive and started down the road. The wipers on his truck didn't work, so we had to move slowly in order to see where we were going. I thought briefly of the old postal saying, "Neither wind nor rain nor dead of night." As we crept down the street, porch lights popped on and a number of people came out of their homes to see what Tat was doing creeping along so slowly with his siren on in the middle of the night.

"Andy knows where the plane is," Tat exclaimed proudly.

That was all it took. By the time we were four streets down we had acquired a nice-sized mob. We were moving slowly enough that those wishing to follow just walked alongside the truck. Because everyone had come directly from their beds to our parade most of them looked like Tat. I had never seen so many grown men in lavender housecoats. I could also see that each person was carrying some sort of object. I figured that they had just grabbed something that looked threatening before they had stepped out of their houses to investigate what all the noise was. I spotted a couple of tennis rackets, a golf club, a fire poker, and a bottle of ketchup. The rain made us look more miserable than we actually felt.

Two streets down we began to lose a few mob members due to the dark night. Ariel slid into the culvert and twisted his ankle. Bryan Find ran directly into the Moore's mailbox, cutting up his right hand pretty bad. Tat just couldn't stand to see his people suffer. He stopped the mail truck and got out. He threw up the back door of the vehicle and reached in. Dim lightning flickered, giving me a shallow view of two cases of Phyllis's Triple Sour Pears.

"Phyllis wanted me to deliver these to Shirlene Hickens but I figure she won't mind if we used a few jars," Tat shouted above the light rain as he passed the jars to the crowd.

"Are we going to eat them?" Mark Tart asked in confusion.

Tat answered by taking off his right shoe and pulling off his sock. He opened a jar of pears and stuffed his sock into it. Then he pulled out a lighter from the first-aid kit he had packed in the back of his mail truck and lit the sock. It produced a great flame. The whole crowed "woooooooed." People began ripping sleeves or pulling off socks and shoving them into the pear jars. Tat happily and heartily lit anything anyone leaned his way. After everyone was illuminated by the light of the burning pears, Tat whistled.

"Let's head 'em out!"

We pressed on. I began to grow a little worried. Actually, that is not true. I was petrified. When I had awakened a few minutes ago it had been my intention for Tat and I to slip over to Pitt's place and discover the truth. Now we had half the town with us, all of them playing with fire and having no idea what they were up to.

We pulled up to Pitt's place and I got out. The crowd grew quiet. I stepped up to the front door with Gordon and Tat while the rest of the mob circled around us as if we were preparing to carol.

"Now what?" Gordon asked.

"I'll knock," I said.

"What if he's sleeping?" Tat worried.

"We're an angry mob," Gordon reminded him.

"Someone knock on the door," Wilson Phelps hollered from behind.

I turned to do so, but before I could get a knock in, the door pulled open to reveal a puzzled-looking Pitt in pajamas and a nightcap.

He stared at us all for a moment and then asked, "What is going on?"

"Andy knows where the plane is," someone yelled.

"Really," Pitt scowled. "And what does that have to do with me?"

"Actually I was hoping we might have this conversation in private." I suddenly wasn't as sure of myself as I had been earlier.

"Well, this seems like a weird way to orchestrate a private conversation," Pitt said.

"They just followed us," I explained.

"So where's the plane, Andy?" he asked, having fully lost his patience with me.

I composed myself and let it fly. "I think you've hidden it."

The crowd gasped.

Pitt smiled coldly. "Where would I hide a plane?"

"Under one of your gravel piles."

"Of course." I could hear a few mob members slap their foreheads, surprised that they hadn't thought of that before. "It's got to be!"

"This is ridiculous," Pitt scoffed. "Why would I want to hide that plane?"

"You needed Reinhold's curse to be true," I said. "If this town ever really grew you would lose too much of your hold." I know my reasoning wasn't particularly solid, but my dream had revealed it all to me.

"That's outrageous."

"I don't know," Bryan Find stepped up. "I don't think anyone's ever looked under your piles."

"And nobody ever will!"

"What's to hide?" Gordon asked.

Everyone seemed surprised by Gordon's backbone. I figured that an evening with Lauren could make almost anyone overly self-assured.

"Yeah," a couple mob members yelled. "What's to hide?"

"This is your doing, Andy," Pitt said angrily.

"The council asked me to find the plane," I said.

"Find the plane!" the mob hollered.

"Maybe we should all just calm down," Tat said.

"Calm down!" the crowd screamed, waving their burning torches.

"I'll call the authorities if you touch one single rock," Pitt said.

It was a silly threat seeing how most of the town's authorities were members of our mob.

"If the plane's not under your gravel then why would you care if we looked?" Gordon asked boldly.

"Look, look, look," the mob chanted. A couple of people broke off and pushed through the gates running to piles of stone and beginning to dig with whatever they could find. Vinton discovered a pile of shovels by tripping over them. He eagerly shared his discovery and in no time at all everyone was tossing gravel and dirt like mad.

"You'll pay for this, Andy," Pitt threatened as he stepped back into his house. "You'll pay for every stone that is misplaced this night." He slammed the door and shut us out.

"I hope you're right about this," Tat said.

I would have been really worried if it had not been for the inspiration that had helped me figure it all out. "It's here," I said with confidence.

Tat and I both grabbed shovels and began digging. We had a mystery to uncover.

CHAPTER TWENTY-EIGHT

OOPS

Morning brought two things: clear skies and rock solid proof that there was no plane under any of Pitt's gravel. A few people still dug at piles too small to properly hide even the tiniest of planes. The mob's enthusiasm had diminished considerably. Some folks were actually sleeping on the edge of the gravel yard and everyone was covered in mud. I sat down on a long railroad tie and put my head in my hands. Tat wandered over and took a seat right next to me.

"Where should we dig next, Andy?" he asked.

"The plane's not here," I said.

I think Tat was going to do some minor scolding, but he was interrupted by the sight of Pitt stepping out from his house and crossing over towards us all. Those who noticed him stood and looked anywhere besides directly his way.

"Well, well, well," Pitt smiled. "As I live and grieve. It sure is neighborly of you all to come out here and rip apart my business. Did you find what you were looking for?" His thin body

seemed to quiver under the tiny breeze the morning was coughing up.

If people weren't looking at him before, they were even
more not looking at him now.

"I suppose it was easier to listen to Andy, who has only been
here for a short while, than to me," he went on. "I guess my living alongside you for all this time means nothing. Well, I'm
sickened."

A couple of people coughed.

"Pitt's right," Bryan Find said. "What's he ever done to make
us not trust him?"

"It is awful sad the way we turned on him so fast," Gordon
admitted.

"It's Andy's fault," someone pointed out.

"Yeah," a number of muddy men agreed.

"Wait a second," I attempted to explain. "I didn't . . ."

"Andy's fault!" everyone yelled with reinvigorated mob-like
mentality.

"We were tricked," Mark Tart yelled.

"Tricked!" they all screamed.

"Listen, I'm not . . ."

Tat interrupted me by taking my arm and whispering,
"You'd better get out of here. I'd hate for this mob to get any
uglier than it already is."

I looked at everyone and wondered if that was actually possible. I wanted to explain myself, but I also wanted to live to see
the next couple of days. I stepped through the crowd hoping
that someone would stop me and tell me that they knew this
wasn't entirely my fault. No one did. I walked alone down the
muddy drive and back towards the Harding house.

Heaven had helped me make one huge mistake.

Phyllis was sticking mail in boxes when I walked in covered with mud and more depressed than I may ever have been before. She turned, offering me a glimpse of her half glasses and full smile.

"Andy, honey," she tisked. "Are you all right?"

"No."

"I heard about the lack of plane," she said sympathetically. "Farleen Lace just called and gave me the details."

"I blew it."

"We all have off days," Phyllis said. "If it makes you feel any better, Summer called and wanted me to tell you that she has to make a run to Moab. She won't be back until after the carnival tomorrow."

I stared at her wondering how in the world that bit of news should make me feel better.

"She's thinking of you," she added.

I walked the long stairs up to my room and fell deep onto the pink bed that I had grown overly accustomed to. I looked at the purple vanity as I lay flat against the comforter. Light filtered in through the white-paned window like glitter. What was I doing here? How could I have just kept right on walking deeper into this place? There had been plenty of times earlier on when it would have seemed almost natural to turn and pull away. Now, however, I was a regular. A confused, dimwitted, underachieving local who knew no more than those who sat next to me on any given day.

Stupid plane.

Pitt.

Inspiration and its insatiable need to make me humble.

I had been so sure. Last night the possibility of Pitt hiding the plane had been so obvious. I knew with everything in me that he had been behind its disappearance. It was as if my entire life had been lived so that my brain would be capable of figuring it out at just that moment. My brain had been horribly wrong.

I turned myself over and stared at the ceiling.

"Hello," I spoke, wondering if the cosmos were aware of me at the moment. The white slat ceiling remained closed-lipped and guarded. I blew out as if somewhere someone had just tightly squeezed a doll made in my likeness. Thoughts of my sophomore year in high school played across my memory like an outdated movie. I could see the thick red encyclopedia I had bought at Stevenson's Paper and Pens. It had been an essential prop in a clever idea. For months I had desired to ask Tara Mendoza out on a date. For an equal amount of time I had been unable to work up the courage to do so. Tara was pretty and sat two desks over from me in social studies. She had an older brother named Brad and a pony that her family housed out in the country. Her laugh was like acceptance from the most popular group in school, and her smile seemed to warm even the worst of the cafeteria's lunches.

I probably never would have been bold enough to make a move if it had not been for the brilliant idea fate seemed to dump in my lap. One night while I was drifting off to sleep I came up with the thought of buying a dictionary and doctoring it just a bit so as to make Tara think I was clever. I bought the book, whited out the definition of romance, and wrote "See Andy Phillips" in its place. I circled the new definition and wrinkled the page a bit so that the book would easily open up to it. I then delivered it to her in person. She took it, thanked me, and never spoke to me again. I heard through the grapevine that the wrinkled page had not done its part. She never saw my alteration. Instead she went around telling all her friends about the creepy kid that gave girls encyclopedias. A year later I saw the very book I had given her in the school library. When no one was around I looked up romance. Someone had written in "Avoid," in front of my name. I came into my own about six months later, and all those I had once desired to impress seemed silly and not worthwhile. Still, it had always bugged me that some part of me had whispered to do what I had done. Then when I did just that, a greater cosmic force had made sure that my effort went anywhere besides where I had planned. My attempt to woo Tara had been no different than my attempt to prove Pitt guilty.

I had failed.

I would have spent a bit longer feeling sorry for myself but sleep seemed to roll in with the sullen mood. It began to smother any and all resolve I had to stay awake. The long night I had just been through was taking its toll. Images of Tara Mendoza and my sophomore year hairstyle got in the parting thought.

CHAPTER TWENTY-NINE

SHAKING THINGS UP

It took a while after Thunder City was founded to discover what it was good at. Corn came in short, beans grew tiny, and the east Thunder City rice paddies were a total failure altogether. Shortly into the history of the town, Marcus Tart received a letter from his uncle in Idaho. His uncle went on and on about how rewarding and profitable potato farming was. Marcus wrote back and within a couple months he had received another letter from his uncle explaining how to do everything connected with spud mining. Folks planted and prayed. Hopes were high about having finally found something to bring the town a real economy. Stan Frank gave a stirring talk one week at church challenging everyone to show God just how much faith they had in a bountiful crop by building the biggest potato cellars they could.

"If we build them, God will fill them," Stan had promised.

People liked the idea. Everyone set about constructing the largest cellars they could build. The Tarts built seven; the Backers nine. And the Franks built twelve, each one double the size of any of the others. At the completion of the cellars the seasons cooperated by bringing about harvesttime. Sadly, it didn't take more than a couple of hours to discover that there was no way that the entire town's bounty would fill even one of the cellars. People had failed to find out before building just how successful or unsuccessful potato growing was in their part of the country. They knew now that even their faith couldn't turn the soil in Thunder City into the type of dirt that potatoes yearned for.

A few of the cellars were torn down. Two of the Tart's were used to store cattle, and the Frank's largest became an indoor dump that had reached full capacity years ago. The rest had simply sat there weathering the elements and longing for some sort of purpose.

The following morning I received two very bothersome pieces of paper. One was an invitation on colored construction paper with scissor-trimmed edges and a green piece of yarn tied into a bow at the corner. As festive as the invitation was, it didn't excite me to receive it seeing how it was a request for me to appear before the Council of Seven the following night at nine.

"Phyllis thought I should make it look pretty so as to soften the blow," Tat explained as he handed it to me.

"Thanks."

Tat had more for me.

"What is it?" I asked, taking the white piece of folded paper he was holding.

"Darndest thing," Tat laughed. "I guess that little dig we did two nights ago really upset Pitt."

"He's suing me?" I complained, after having read the first few lines of the summons Tat had handed me.

"Some folks bruise easy."

"Tat," I complained. "He's suing me."

"I'm sure it can be worked out."

"Of my hide."

"That's the attitude," he encouraged, not understanding what I just said.

"I guess I need a lawyer," I said.

Tat coughed suspiciously.

"Do you know one?" I asked.

"Let's just say I could have put a fifth plaque on my door."

"You?" I asked in amazement. "You're a lawyer?"

"What can I say?" Tat blushed with embarrassment. "I was young and got sucked into the flashy life of litigation."

There were any number of remarks I could have made regarding what he had just said. Unfortunately I just didn't have it in me to be sarcastic and clever at the moment.

"My fees are reasonable," he informed me.

"I'll tell you what. I'll give you everything I have left once Pitt gets through with me."

"Deal," Tat smiled while extending his hand to shake mine.

I read the local paper while eating breakfast with Tat. Every page was filled with facts and pictures concerning Pitt and his disappointment in humankind. The Mayor of Mishap was having to sue one of the locals for persecution and compensation. It was an enlightening read. There was a picture of me on page two. Unfortunately it was the one where I was blinking into the camera. Apparently Tat had slipped into my room while I was sleeping and snatched it.

"I didn't want to disturb you," Tat explained.

"Oh," I replied, thinking about how he had done just that.

There was an article talking about the carnival that was being held today. Above the article was a picture of last year's pie eating contest for local charities.

"Why aren't you at the carnival?" I asked Tat.

"It's too hot. Besides, I don't care for crowds. Phyllis is out there representing us. Her pears should win us another ribbon. But listen, Andy," he went on, obviously wanting to talk about other things than the carnival. "We've got to go at Pitt strong. This lawsuit will be tough."

"I agree," I said putting the paper down. "So have you got any dirt on him?"

"Now, we don't want to be mean," Tat said sincerely.

We were going to be slaughtered.

"So you really think Pitt will go through with this?"

"I do," he said. "He even held a press conference last night down in his potato cellars. "He claims he's only doing it for the victims that come after him."

"He owns those potato cellars?" I asked.

"All the ones west of East Fourth Street."

"Of course," I whispered as the answer I had been seeking hit me.

"I'm glad you believe me," Tat said.

Finally fate and I were on the same page. Heaven was lining up the answers for me. Every single one of those potato cellars was large enough to house a plane. Perhaps I made a sorry Captain Matrimony, but I appeared to have promise as Detective Amazing. There was no way heaven would lead me astray twice.

"Do you know where Pitt is now?" I asked with excitement.

"I'm sure he's out at the carnival," Tat answered. "He sets up a Meet the Mayor booth each year. He also gives a speech and passes out chocolate coins."

"Do you want to go see the plane?" I asked with excitement.

"Andy, don't you think . . ."

"This time I'm positive about where it is."

"But Andy . . ."

"Look, I know I blew it before. But this time it's different."

"I'm not sure about this," Tat said nervously. "It makes me a little Larry."

"A little *Larry* or a little *leery*?" I asked.

Tat looked at me as though he thought I had been attempting to yodel.

"Besides," I went on. "What have you got to lose? If I'm wrong, I'll just have to hire you for my second trial."

Now Tat smiled. "Let's go."

I didn't need convincing.

CHAPTER THIRTY

AND THEN THEY WERE DONE

Thunder City held its first Annual City Carnival in the summer of 1943. It was not a tremendous success. The total attendance for the day was eleven. The following year they decided to add food and games to the event and the attendance shot up to twenty-four. Two years later with the addition of musicians and pony rides the carnival had finally arrived. These days if there were ever a complaint it was usually that nothing fun ever happened there and that it was always the same old same old.

It was stupid, I know, but I had to do it. I couldn't just sit around and wait for Pitt's lawsuit to ruin me. I also knew that I had to move fast or Pitt might find a way to move the plane. I'd just have to swallow my pride and confront him. The answer was so clear in my mind this time that I couldn't deny what I knew.

We raced through the town in Tat's vehicle with the windows down. A tremendous heat was settling and making the air feel like it belonged in Phoenix instead of Mishap. At the edge of town we turned and flew down the wide road that ended at Knock Pond. From a distance I could see that a huge crowd had turned out for the carnival. A number of striped tents had been set up as well as a couple of rides. I spotted a small pony pull that had been assembled in the far corner of the festivities. Tat braked hard, allowing the dirt that had been trailing us to blow over. I coughed and waved as I stepped out of the car. Tat rushed to my side.

"I hope you're right about this." He was worried.

"Me too."

People were everywhere. There was music coming from a small group of bearded men with fiddles and guitars. The smells and sounds of summer filled the air. I wiped my forehead and wondered how anybody could be having fun in this heat. I spotted Bert and Annie Lawson over by the "Guess Your Weight" booth. Annie was on the scale smiling. I watched the gentleman running the booth say something to her. The smiling ceased and Annie ran off crying. Chad Tinderhawkins was spending his hard-earned paper route money on darts to throw in the balloon game. I could see a big radio at the top of the prize pyramid and had no doubt about what he was aiming for.

"This is big," I said to Tat. "I had no idea so much effort was going to be put into this."

"It sure has grown over the years."

I looked around trying to spot Pitt's booth while walking down the main row of tents. "Let's just find Pitt and get this over with," I said to nobody, seeing how I had lost Tat a good seven steps back thanks to the call of the caramel apple vendor.

I stopped and waited for him. When he finally came back he had a caramel-looking goatee and bits of red in his teeth.

"Care for a bite?" he offered.

I politely declined. As we walked past the animal tents I couldn't help but notice that all the livestock seemed jumpy and nervous.

"Don't those ponies look a little anxious?" I asked Tat.

"Hey, if you were faced with the possibility of some of these folks sitting on you, wouldn't you be? Besides, this heat would make any animal skittish."

Just beyond the animals, Nick Goodfellow's Tunnel of Love sat perched over a full canal. I could see a few people floating on tubes through the tent Nick had set up. The water looked extremely inviting on such a hot day. I wished Summer were here so that we could cement our relationship by drifting together.

We strode past Nick's place and over to Lilith Stern's Avon kiosk. Lilith welcomed us with a bright made-up smile and melting cosmetics. She had on an orange dress that was checkered with mustard-yellow pineapples.

"Have you seen Pitt, Lil?" Tat asked her.

"He should be right over there past the cotton candy wagon," she nodded.

"Selling much?" Tat asked her, as an afterthought.

"Oh sure." Lilith fanned herself. "This kind of atmosphere makes everyone want to look beautiful."

I could tell Tat was tempted to stay and see if she had anything that might make him feel prettier. Luckily he suppressed those desires and walked off toward the cotton candy wagon with me. Pitt was not around. There was, however, a tall stool and small table set up with banners that read: Meet the Mayor.

I made a remark about truth in advertising, and Tat commented on how one caramel apple didn't really fill a person up.

I was edgy, hot, and uncomfortable. I knew where the plane was and my best shot at clearing this whole thing up was to confront Pitt publicly. Tat and I helped ourselves to two corn dogs, a giant pretzel, and a couple huge wads of cotton candy as we contemplated what our next move should be.

"So where *is* the plane?" Tat asked for the fiftieth time.

"Let's find Pitt first."

The fact that Pitt was not around made me think that maybe he had read my mind—that he was at this very moment disposing of the plane. I couldn't afford to be wrong again. Everything I liked about Mishap would be ruined if I were wrong about this.

Nick Goodfellow spotted Tat and me and asked if we had gotten a chance to go through the Tunnel of Love. We swore that we were interested, but that since Tat and I had come together instead of with our sweethearts we were going to pass. Nick hurried off to invite more people to partake of his creation.

Just as I was beginning to feel the effect of eating too much carnival food, the crowds began to swell and move towards the amphitheater. Tat and I figured that Pitt would probably be where the people were, so we followed the crowd. The reason for the gathering was that everyone wanted to witness firsthand the Mishap annual charity pie eating contest. In front of the crowd sat eight people with plastic bibs on. Rick Tew, the MC, was still trying to recruit more people to make fools of themselves. We stopped in the middle of the crowd right next to a dejected looking Chad Tinderhawkins. I noticed the small stuffed bear he held in his right hand.

"Anyone else?" Rick asked the crowd. "It's for a good cause." He spotted Tat standing by me and publicly challenged us both to take part.

"I'm full," Tat hollered back.

Rick and a large part of those in attendance began making chicken noises at us. The next thing I knew Tat had pulled me by the elbow through the crowd and was handing me a plastic bib.

"I'm not doing this," I argued, as everyone clapped and chanted.

"If I have to then so do you," Tat hollered back.

"You don't have to," I pointed out.

"I don't know how folks live back east, Andy. But here we have a little thing called honor," Tat scolded as he stood there in a vinyl bib that read: Spit Happens. "We can't just let those chicken noises go unchallenged."

How could I argue that? I sat down dejectedly behind the long table and in front of a huge pile of pies. Tat sat next to me and smiled.

"It's not like we're being forced to travel across America in a handcart," he pointed out.

"People didn't ride in the handcarts," I complained. "They pulled them."

"Exactly," Tat said, positioning himself for maximum pie intake.

Rick Tew explained the rules and then told us about a new aspect of the annual pie eating contest.

"The person who eats the least amount of pie gets to man the dunk tank."

Perfect. I had been planning to just go through the motions but now I actually had to eat or else I would have to spend the rest of the afternoon being dunked. Before I could get in an adequate amount of self-pity Rick hollered, "Go!"

I stuck my face in the first pie and pushed the pan around trying to shove as much of the chocolate mess as I could into my mouth. The filling pushed into my eyes, hair, and nose. I tossed the first pan over and began getting acquainted with another. I couldn't actually see Tat due to the fact that my face was pressed into a pie tin. But I could tell by the bits of food that were hitting me from his direction that he was making some real time.

The crowd was going crazy.

"Go! Go! Go!"

I heard someone scream their support for Trevor Moore by yelling, "Slurp 'em down, Trevor!"

I finished my third pie and dove into number four. My stomach reminded me that it was there, and that it had been quite full before all the pie, thank you very much. I ignored it and went on. Wilson Phelps was sitting next to me on the right. He signaled his defeat by moaning and then falling backwards. Half a pie later, Bert, who was sitting two seats over, collapsed face first into the very same pie that had done him in. Flecks were flying from Tat's direction letting me know that he was still going strong. People screamed and clapped as Rick broad-casted who was in the lead and how far ahead the leader was. I couldn't hear him very clearly due to all the pudding in my ears, but I was able to make out that I wasn't the loser. Knowing that, and having no desire to be the winner, I stopped where I was. I fingered pie out of my eyes and looked over at Tat. He was so covered in pie that I could barely make out the features of his head. He just looked like a body with a large glop of goo as his noggin.

Tat came in second.

"Sorry you didn't win," I said to the mound of muck on top of Tat's neck.

"Hey, at least I got seven free pies."

There is always a silver lining.

As we were trying to wipe ouselves off, Tat noticed Pitt walking back behind the crowd. He leaned into me and whispered. We slipped away from the festivities in hopes of catching up to our mayor. I would have preferred to confront Pitt pie free and with a bit more dignity, but there was no time to properly clean up.

We caught up with Pitt at his booth. He was out in front of those gathered, preparing to make a speech. I walked up to him and asked if he could spare a moment. He looked at my pudding-covered face and said, "No."

"I know where you have the plane," I whispered.

He turned slowly and gave me a wicked grin. "You just don't give up, do you? What is it now? Is there something else of mine that you want to tear apart?"

It was hard for me to take any of this too seriously due to the strong scent of chocolate pie I was emitting. But I tried my best to make my point.

"Pitt, I know about the cellars," I said calmly.

"What?" he said a little agitated.

A couple of people sitting nearby were listening in. I figured that the most effective way for this to come about was to just get it out in the open.

"I know where the plane is," I announced to the small crowd.

A few people laughed, having known about my previous attempt to explain the mystery.

"This time I'm certain."

"Andy," Pitt sneered.

A couple more people stopped to listen to what I was saying.

"I was told to find the plane and I have," I announced. "And you might all like to know how your mayor figures into this." From the few expressions I could see, they did. Those in attendance leaned in to hear what I was going to say next.

"It seems . . ."

I have confessed quite candidly that I do not understand how and why heaven does what it does. I suppose those in the spiritual know might be able to predict when God is going to touch down and make miracles. Or maybe no one really knows, thus keeping life interesting and unpredictable. Either way, I could not have been more surprised by the sudden movement of the earth. It was small, but there was no denying that the ground beneath our feet had shimmied.

The entire carnival was silent for a brief second as we all tried to digest what we had just experienced. Tat held his hands up as if to calm the already subdued. Before he could say anything, however, the world rocked again. It was harder this time, actually throwing a couple of people off balance and to the ground.

There was no silence now.

People began to scream and run as a third quake ripped across the earth like a cosmic gopher bent on burrowing. A huge striped tent toppled. The stakes in the ground jiggled like wet noodles. The large grill at the barbecue cart tipped into the booth where Phyllis was selling her bottled pears. The fruit burst into flame. Pitt darted behind the crafts booth as quilts and scrapbooking supplies tumbled to the ground. I could feel the heat as it seemed to build under the activity of the earth.

A fourth quake shook long and hard. I saw the small log ride begin to break apart and water burst from its base. I looked around desperately trying to remember what you were supposed to do in the event of an earthquake. I decided to just get as far away as I could from the portable wall I was standing by. It felt like I was running across a trampoline, the ground was swelling and stretching so rapidly. I heard a tremendous noise coming from Knock Pond as water broke through the west side and began to soak the shaky ground. Georgia Loft ran past me in a blur, her uneven shoulders looking almost straight thanks to all the shaking.

"Tat!" I hollered, at the same time realizing what a sad state I was in that I was calling for him in the face of danger.

There was no sign of Tat. The only thing I could see was hundreds of people spilling about like giraffes on an ice rink—that, and the end of the world.

CHAPTER THIRTY-ONE

LOOK HARDER

I t was 1924 when Thunder City first discovered that it was
sitting smack dab on the edge of a great fault. The discovery was made when the earth wiggled slightly, tripping
Otis Tart so he stumbled into his own well and cracking the
stucco on the back wall of the city courthouse. To a few, the discovery was further proof that Thunder City wasn't as blessed
as they had originally thought. To the majority, however, the
wobbling ground was a great reminder of the fact that they
really weren't as in control of their lives as they liked to think.
Saints that had been lukewarm got their act together, and the
town went through a true spiritual renewal. It was such a great
change that few histories ever referred to it as the period of the
big quake. Most accounts simply called it the time of great
growth.

God kept the earth still for many years after that.

Mishap was in total and complete shock. Some had known that the city sat on a fault, but the fault had been still for as long as anyone could remember. Knock Pond had been at the epicenter of the earthquake, taking the hit harder than anyplace else. Unfortunately, the town's entire population had been out at the carnival when the shaking had occurred. Rides were knocked over and tents toppled. I heard rumors of a broken leg and a concussion. But the biggest problem was that the earthquake had seemed to rip Knock Pond in half. We all just stood there watching the water lower as it forcefully flushed itself into the Wayne River. It was an awesome sight to watch the ground just east of the pond break apart and surge into the Wayne. Sounds like heavy traffic accompanied the fleeing liquid. There was nothing we could do to stop it from going. The Wayne River surged madly as it carried off the innards of Knock Pond.

"What should we do?" Ariel Backer asked for all of us.

I looked around at the downed tents and injured people that were scattered about like wounded beetles. Tat had gotten a gash on his forehead from a falling post that had tagged him as he ran for cover. He was holding a thick stack of yellow paper napkins up to his bleeding head. Nick Goodfellow stumbled up to us looking as white as Pitt's wife's teeth.

"You all right?" I asked.

"I'm fine," he answered. "The love tunnel didn't make it," he added. "The ditch drained while Bishop Hearth and his wife were floating through. They're muddy but they're okay."

Phyllis spotted Tat and ran to him.

"Oh my . . ."

"Oh you . . ."

They were sweet in a sort of an older, awkward way.

Gordon and Lauren made it over to us. I had never seen

Gordon look more scared. He made the white that Nick had turned look dingy and gray.

"Are you okay?" I asked with concern.

Gordon looked at Lauren nervously.

"He thinks this is because of the curse," Lauren said, sounding as if she wasn't sure that it wasn't. "He had just kissed me behind the pony rides and the earth started shaking."

"We've got to get organized," Tat said.

"We need supplies," Phyllis said with worry. "There are a lot of people scraped up and hurt."

"Andy," Tat said, holding his mail truck keys out to me. "In the pantry back home we've got all those seventy-two-hour kits the Relief Society never sold."

"You want me to get them?" I asked, knowing that the kits consisted mainly of granola bars and soup mix.

"I'm not sure how I could say it any plainer." He waved me off. "Hurry."

"Grab the ones in the top floor linen closet too," Phyllis added.

What can I say? I was accustomed to doing as I was told. Let it be known, however, that even in my hurried state I took the time to realize that Pitt was suspiciously absent from all that was going on.

CHAPTER THIRTY-TWO

THE SOUND OF SOME-
THING WRONG

The town of Mishap was almost completely deserted. I spotted a couple of people, but it appeared that the majority of Mishap truly had been out at the carnival. I could see a toppled light post and a port-a-shed in the Tart's backyard that had collapsed due to the earthquake. Two people were standing next to a broken fire hydrant watching the gushing water squirt high into the air. The earthquake had also shattered the new front windows on Gordon's store. I could see bits of glass resting on top of my car that still sat there in front of it.

I pulled up to the Harding house and hurried into the pantry where Tat had said the kits would be. I shoved all of them into a huge black garbage bag and headed out. At the front door I remembered that Phyllis had instructed me to get the supplies in the top floor linen closet as well. I ran up the stairs so quickly that my foot caught on the landing of the second floor and I fell. I would have just picked myself up and kept going, but I could hear noise escaping from behind the very painting Tat and I had gone behind to visit the Council of Seven. It was a faraway sounding noise like a scratch. The scratch was followed by a clank, and the clank was the precursor to a solid thud.

There was somebody or something moving back there.

I pulled the painting forward and quietly twisted the handle on the door behind it. It was locked. Luckily the old door was loose enough to allow me to wiggle my finger through the gap in the frame and release the latch. It swung open silently. I could hear the noise more clearly now. I stepped in and shut the door. I was tempted to holler out and make myself known, but I decided against it until I knew who I was in there with.

With the door closed it was pretty close to pitch black. In the distance I could see a glow coming from down below some stairs. I walked carefully towards the dim light. After I had descended the stairs and climbed through a small door, I noticed a second passage that went up and to the left. I took it thinking that it would bring me closest to the noise. The tunnels and walkways behind the Harding house walls were really quite remarkable. I thought about how fulfilling it must be to have a home with secret passageways.

Halfway up a tiny set of stairs I realized that the sounds I had been hearing had stopped. I held my breath and listened in silence until the sound resumed. I kept going until I reached a long, skinny room with a low ceiling and bumpy walls. The noise seemed to be coming from behind the bricks at the end of the hall. I pushed myself up against the wall and listened. I could hear the sound of something popping, followed by what sounded like a drawer being pulled open. There was rustling and flipping and then the noise of whatever had been pulled open slamming shut. This sequence of sounds continued three times before I worked up the courage to peer around the wall to see what was really going on.

There was some weak light coming from a naked bulb that hung from the ceiling. Along the wall to my right were rows and rows of small, built-in wooden drawers. I counted at least twenty-three rows up and twenty-one across. But the odd wall of drawers wasn't half as interesting as the person who was systematically going through them at the moment.

Pitt.

I watched him pry open one on the bottom row with a short crowbar. He rummaged through it quickly and then slammed it shut. He stopped to look at his watch and then opened the next one. I was greatly tempted to step out of the shadows and catch him red-handed at whatever he was doing. But once again something told me to hold off and wait this one out a moment more. About ten drawers later he discovered some contents that seemed to bring him great joy. He flipped carefully through the files and then laughed gleefully when he came upon something which seemed to please him greatly. He pulled out a single sheet of paper, stared at it under the fuzzy light, and then folded it and put it into his pocket. He then took what looked like my missing watch and dropped it on the floor haphazardly.

I couldn't believe it. I was being framed. Pitt must have used the hidden spaces in the Harding house to sneak around and steal my stuff.

He turned as if to head off in the opposite direction of me. I stepped up quietly behind him and spoke.

"Did you find what you were looking for?"

Pitt could have won a gold medal for the freestanding high jump he executed.

"Andy!"

"What'd you find?"

I watched him try desperately to regain his composure.

"Hand it over," I insisted.

"I don't know what you're talking about," he said, his composure running at about sixty percent.

"The paper, Pitt," I clarified. "The one you'd like everyone else to think I took."

He didn't have to stand there and take this. And he proved that point by darting off into the dark passageway to the left of us.

"Pitt," I hollered. I was now going to have to run after him with my hurt foot. As I ran, the light behind the walls became darker and darker. I thought I was following his trail precisely until I ran headfirst into a very solid wall. As soon as the stars had faded, I felt around for another opening or hallway. I found one to my left and walked down it slowly holding my arms out in front of me. Ten steps further I discovered stairs that led down into a blackness that outer darkness would be envious of. I had no choice but to go down. Eleven steps into my descent I heard from behind me, "I can't let you leave."

This was outer darkness, and Satan had just hissed at me.

"You've been most helpful in providing me a way out of all this," Pitt whispered smugly.

I turned to look towards his voice. "I'm happy to help."

"Funny till the end," he said sarcastically. "I wish I could tell the others that you died with a smile on your face, but to be honest it's just too dark to tell. You know, Andy, I've actually enjoyed toying with you all this time. I voted for you to come teach simply because I needed an outsider to take the blame. You've worked perfectly."

I wasn't sure what he wanted me to say, so I said nothing and he went on. "You see we do things our way here. It's not wrong; it's just our way. I'm actually impressed by how you'll be an important part of my achievement."

Before I could emit any fear, he barreled into me knocking me backwards down the stairs. The force didn't hurt as much as his thin shoulders as they jutted into me. We fell down a full set of stairs. The stars I saw earlier were obviously from a lesser kingdom than the ones that exploded across my mind now. I slammed to a stop at the bottom of the landing, my head wedging in the space between the floor and the wall. I could feel Pitt reaching out trying to find where certain parts of me were. I did my best to help him locate my fist.

I was embarrassed by how little my blow affected him.

Pitt introduced his foot to my lower back while I fought to make him aware of my knee. I could actually feel the air coming out of him as my blow connected. I scrambled to my feet and took off in a hard run. I went all of seventeen inches before I was stopped by another wall.

The dark was doing me in.

I fell to the ground just as Pitt came flying over me and into the wall himself. He slid down on top of me and began scratching. I suddenly didn't feel so wimpy about my soft punch earlier. I pushed him off of me and stood up. I couldn't see, but I could hear him pull himself to his feet as well.

There was relative silence as we both tried to quietly catch our breath. Neither one of us wanted to give away our position. I can say in all honesty that Pitt was doing a bang-up job of keeping his location hidden, seeing how I had no idea where he was. He could have been standing two inches in front of me and I wouldn't have been able to tell thanks to the darkness. But he spoke, letting me know he was at least a few feet over to the right.

"It's no use, Andy," he insisted. "I've been up and down these passages a million times. I have the advantage."

I stepped back slowly, hoping to come up against a wall or an exit.

"You were wrong to have ever come here." Pitt sniffed.

I wondered if he meant come here to Mishap? Or here to the Harding house?

A wall pushed up behind me. I began sliding along it, away from Pitt's voice.

"I've never really lost anything," Pitt bragged.

I was mad that I needed to keep quiet, seeing how I kept thinking of smart-aleck comebacks for the things he was saying.

"I'm certain when the dust settles that I'll come out even more powerful than I am now," he continued.

More powerful than being the mayor of a small Utah town? It was a weak example of one of the sarcastic things I could have been throwing back at him. But I stayed quiet as I inched myself even further away.

I'm not sure whether or not I've mentioned it before, but I'm not a big fan of surprises. I could count at least a dozen surprises that life had thrown me that I had not particularly enjoyed. I can remember my fourteenth birthday and coming home from school to find an empty house. I instantly started cheering and singing to myself about how great it was to not have any overbearing parents home to monitor what I watched on TV or ate out of the fridge. I quickly dialed up and began a phone conversation with a boy my parents had forbidden me to talk to. Just as I started to say a few things about how clueless parents could be, I noticed my Uncle David's head sheepishly rise from behind the far sofa. It was only a second later that I spotted my parents leaning in from another room.

"Surprise!" my Aunt Leslie weakly cheered.

It took me six months to get over that surprise.

Of course even that impromptu experience didn't catch me off guard like the feel of Pitt's hands around my neck, despite the fact that I had just heard him speaking over five feet away from me. I had no idea how he was able to have seen me, or how he managed to grab my neck on his first try. The only plausible explanation I could think of was that he had simply called in a favor from old Scratch himself.

At the moment, however, this was all inconsequential seeing how my air intake was being severely cut off. Apparently Pitt's vocal cords still worked fine because he said, "You were wrong about me, Andy. You thought I was just some bothersome addition to the calculations you've been trying to solve. But I'm more than that, Andy."

I felt that he had made it perfectly clear that he knew my name. Aside from that I had no idea what he was talking about. He pushed me harder up against the wall as if he had read my mind and was bothered by the fact that I didn't understand. I could feel a doorway a couple of feet to the right of us.

"I've got a new purpose in life," he hissed. "I plan to spend the rest of my days convincing people what a horrible and wicked person you were. I, on the other hand, will continue to gain respect and immortality."

Pitt Frank was nuts. His father had been dead-on when he named him Pity. Because at the moment there was nobody I pitied more than him. Except myself, seeing how I was running out of breath.

"I'll tell Summer good-bye for you," he laughed as the core

of his tiny personality finally surfaced. He was the little wooden doll that was so small that no face or detail could be painted onto him. He was spitting mad and ranting about the lies he would soon feed Summer.

I wouldn't have it. I pulled frantically at his hands, but his tight grip seemed locked solid. I kicked and gurgled with all I had in me. I twisted my body in an attempt to pull away towards the opening I could feel. It worked. Unfortunately, the opening was that of a long stairwell. With Pitt still clinging to me, we both went flying down the stairs. I could feel elbows and knees prodding and pummeling me as the two of us bumped down the steps. My head hit the wall at least four times before we came to a stop with a tremendous thud.

Fortunately for me, Pitt had absorbed most of my impact. I rolled off of him and tried to get to my feet as fast as possible. He didn't seem to be doing the same. I slowly caught my breath and then reached my foot out to feel if he was still there. He was, and he wasn't moving.

"Pitt?"

Nothing.

I knew I was doing a dumb thing, but I did it anyway. I got down on my knees and felt around for his head. I never realized he had such big nostrils before. I held my hand over his mouth to see if I could feel him breathing. It was hard to tell. I put my hand on his chest in hopes of feeling movement. There could have been some, but I was so shaky at the moment that it was difficult to tell whether it was him or me.

I got back up and started in on the impossible task of finding a way out. It took me ten minutes and two sets of stairs before I discovered a long tunnel that ran straight for much longer than the Harding property took up. I figured it had to lead somewhere with less stairs and darkness.

I was right. It came out behind the mop closet in the church building. I was incredibly impressed with all the digging that must have been done at some point in the past. I stepped out of the mop closet and into the dimly lit hall of the ward house. I ran quickly to the front door and released the lock that let me out. Because of the dark tunnels I had forgotten that it was broad daylight. The shine of the outdoors made me put my hands up as if an alien in a bright flashy ship was just now landing.

I ran all the way back to the Harding house. I wasn't about to go back in and retrieve the supplies I had originally been sent to get for fear that Pitt would be standing behind the door ready to finish me off. So I jumped into the mail truck and sped faster than any local laws allowed.

I couldn't wait to tell everyone everything I knew. Pitt was hurt. Pitt was guilty. Of what exactly I still wasn't sure, but he had been in the process of framing me which meant that he was definitely a bad guy. Not to mention the fact that he had tried to kill me.

Pitt had the plane in one of his potato cellars and he probably knew what had happened to Larry and Tillie.

I tried not to feel too excited since on the whole it had been a rather terrible day.

CHAPTER THIRTY-THREE

PLANE AS DAY

Knock Pond was so much more than just a source of water. It was the social hub of Thunder City. People swam in it, fished in it, and lay round it like the high mark on a receding lake. There had been outdoor concerts held on its shores, swimming merit badges earned in its waters, and kisses stolen beneath the sunsets and scents that it so beautifully helped nature embellish. From the moment Mayor Buck Moore had first signed the papers that brought it about to the present day, it was a source of great pride and enjoyment.

Of the many attributes and highlights Knock Pond possessed, the very favorite of most was the scene it caused when a full moon was hovering over it. Because the water was so clear, the light of a fat moon pushed easily to the bottom of the pond, causing the minerals and rocks within the dirt to shimmer like diamonds. The very best place to witness this miracle of nature was perched atop Lop Rock. Children and adults would crowd the rock and gaze in wonder at the beauty of their pond.

In the late 1920s there was some discussion about expanding Knock Pond. Advocates argued that if it was this beautiful now, it would be twice as beautiful bigger. It was put to a vote and passed. Unfortunately, the effort involved in making it larger required much more energy and money than simply organizing a vote. No one had it in them to make it happen, and Knock Pond remained its original size. Not including the drought of '67 when its level receded a full six feet during late summer.

When I pulled back up to the fallen carnival I was surprised to discover how organized Tat and Phyllis had gotten things. There was a tent for those with scrapes; a tent for the bruised, swollen, and broken; and a tent for the confused and fearful. (I couldn't help but notice how much more the last tent was bulging.) I found Tat in the Tent of Fear and informed him that I had not gotten the things he needed.

"It took you that long to come up empty?" he asked as he moved to another victim. He felt her forehead as if fear were something that manifested itself in a low-grade fever.

"Tat, I've got to talk to you," I insisted.

"Andy, there are people hurting here."

"It's about Pitt," I blurted out. "He was in your house going through some of the council drawers."

"What?" Tat asked, finally giving me his full attention.

"He was looking for something."

"What something?"

"I have no idea, but he found it and was trying to frame me. We fought about it and I think he may be hurt."

"Andy, this is serious," Tat said, pulling both of us away from listening ears. "Those council drawers are sacred."

"Well he wasn't exactly revering them when I caught him," I whispered loudly. "He's a bad guy, Tat. He hid the plane and now he was trying to do me in."

"Did he tell you where the plane was?" Tat asked excitedly.

"No, but I know where it is."

"Where?"

"He hid it in . . ."

I heard a loud voice from outside the tent and over towards the pond begin shouting.

"The plane!" I heard someone yell. "It's the plane!"

The earthquake had nothing up on the rumbling everyone created while running to see what was going on. People were all over outside pointing towards the pond and hollering. Tat and I crested the banks of the draining pond and stood there slack-jawed and mystified. There—stuck deep in the floor of the shallow part of Knock Pond—was what looked to be the long, flat wings of a small plane. Tat turned and looked at me as if in awe.

"You were right," he whispered.

"Actually," I started to explain.

"Andy was right!" he hollered to the crowd.

"I . . ." I didn't have the heart to tell him that I had never suspected such a thing. I had thought the plane was tucked away in one of Pitt's potato cellars.

"Andy knew it was down there," Bryan Find declared.

The water continued to recede while we all just stood there staring. I was surprised by how wide and long the wings were. Though they were muddy, I could see that the paint on them was dissolving, creating splotchy designs across their span. It struck me that with stormy waters to kick up the pond bottom, and a full moon to reflect from the wings, it might just have been possible for the plane to create an image across the water. I wondered if anyone else was thinking the same thing.

The break in the pond reached its limit and finally stopped sharing what it had with the Wayne River. Bishop Hearth and Jeff Moore climbed down into the pond and pushed through the mud. I was wondering what they were doing until they got to the plane and began to dig. I had forgotten that the aircraft had been carrying passengers when it had gone down. The entire crowd held its breath as a few more people crawled through the mud and helped dig. After what seemed like an eternity Bishop Hearth stood and called, "It looks empty!"

"Ohhhs," "Awwwws," and "Oh, my goodnesses," rang through the air. The plane had been found, but the Cutlers were still missing. The bishop and the others continued to dig, wanting to make sure that there really was no sign of Larry and Tillie.

"What about Pitt?" I asked Tat, remembering that I had left him alone and hurt.

Tat responded by rounding up a few willing people to come with us. Together we found Pitt still lying right where I'd left him. He regained a sort of consciousness as we drove him over to the Thunder City community hospital. We retrieved the piece of paper that he had stolen, but what was written on it didn't seem to clear anything up. It looked to be simply a formula for mixing and making paint. Vinton Moore stayed with Pitt to make sure that he wasn't offered any opportunity to get away before he could explain what he had been up to. We left Vinton and Pitt at the hospital and drove back out to the pond.

As soon as we got there Tat and I jumped down into the muck and began helping all those still working on getting the plane out. It was dark before any very effective equipment arrived to help in the excavation. Pulleys and trucks tugged until a huge sucking sound indicated that the earth was finally willing to give up the goods.

Everyone cheered as the ruins of the plane scraped across the pond bottom and up onto the banks. People flocked around it as if it were a lone TV broadcasting the secret formula to prosperity.

I tried to channel my thoughts elsewhere. If the plane was here, where were Larry and Tillie? My thoughts were interrupted by the voice questioning me from behind.

"Andy?"

I turned to find Maggie Hearth looking lightly muddy and fairly attractive. She had her hair done differently and was wearing an outfit that fit the occasion.

"I've been wanting to talk to you," she admitted sheepishly.

I considered pretending like I hadn't heard her, but instead I said, "What's up?"

"Thanks for talking to Burton the other night." She smiled. "He was really down."

"It was nothing."

"And thanks for pushing me away."

"I didn't do anything."

"He's a different man ever since you talked with him. He's looking for a job that will keep him home more often," she said. She seemed excited and relieved.

"I'm glad."

I was about to say something else bland and relatively harmless when she leaned in and kissed me on the ear. She pulled away, waved, and then walked off. I stared after her until I heard, "So this is what you do when I leave?"

I turned around to find Summer standing there in a clean

T-shirt and shorts and looking at me as if I were underdressed for the occasion. Sure, I still had pie in my ears and hair as well as mud covering my bottom half, not to mention the beginnings of bruises from my encounter with Pitt. But in the eyes of the Creator are we not all created equal?

"Maggie was thanking me," I defended myself.

Summer pushed her hair behind her ears and gave me a full view of her blue eyes. "So it looks like you had a wild day." She glanced around at the mild chaos that was finally beginning to simmer down.

"You should have been here," I smiled, happy to be talking about something besides Maggie and Burton. "It was one heck of a carnival."

"I heard. Did you win me a goldfish?" she asked.

"No, but I almost threw up five pies."

I know that everything was completely unconducive to kissing at the moment, but amidst all the chaos and confusion nature seemed to be pulling Summer and me together. Maybe it was the fact that I had almost died today that attracted her to me despite my pie-filled ears. Or maybe the short absence had made her heart grow so much fonder of me that the threat of mud was not only tolerable, but overlooked.

I looked at the dark sky. Was it me or had the North Star just signaled for me to kiss her? Obviously, it was just me, seeing how the second I moved in to kiss her, she pulled back.

"You weren't trying to kiss me, were you?" she laughed.

"No." It was a clever recovery.

"I'll tell you what. If you wash off your left hand I might loosely hold your pinky," she offered.

I was determined to do more than lock pinkies. I looked into her eyes and stepped up right next to her.

"You wouldn't."

I did. The carnival, the plane, Pitt, Mishap and all that it brought with it fell away like barnacles from Teflon. I put my arms around her and kept the kiss alive by whispering just how much I had missed her.

She missed me back.

When I finally pulled away the air seemed overflowing with oxygen and Summer had a personal testimony of the fact that it had been chocolate pie in the pie-eating contest.

"I'm mad about this," she whispered, referring to the messy kiss. But she was smiling.

"Let's see if we can upgrade that to angry."

The plane was examined, the carnival cleared, loose animals were collected, and the heavens were happy as two souls signaled that male and female were still very much in awe of each other.

CHAPTER THIRTY-FOUR

HERO IN A WAY

There was a long list of things that Mishap needed to repair. The quake had left us broken and torn in a lot of ways. The pond and the water system had to be reengineered and rebuilt. The trust that folks had in their elected officials had plummeted thanks to Pitt. The city courthouse had lost a section of the west wing roof. Gordon's store windows were shattered. A crack was found in the Hasting house foundation.

Etc. Etc. Etc.

The one thing that I felt needed repair more than anything else was also the very thing that was never going to get it. Not that I hadn't tried to fix it, mind you, but there is only so much whining one man can do. The irreparable defect that would never be corrected was the fact that everyone thought I had solved the plane case. I tried to tell people that I didn't discover the plane; the heavens had. But everyone just laughed and then asked in all seriousness, "So when did you first suspect it was there?"

Or they said with complete honesty, "Oh I get it, the gravel dig was just a ploy to get Pitt off track."

Or they wrote into the local paper, "Our city would still be in confusion and disarray without the sharp tack we call Andy Phillips."

The plane, the earthquake, and the arrest of Pitt made national news. I had people from TV shows that were actually respected call me up and plead with me for an interview. I considered accepting one of the offers and then telling the whole world that I had thought the plane was in Pitt's potato cellar. Instead, I figured I would just pull back as much as possible and let it all blow over. I prayed for a new war or a huge natural disaster to take people's attention away from our story.

There was only one perk to all the confusion. It seemed that all the exposure got our story to places it may never have reached without it. I didn't realize the full impact of this until about a week after the earthquake. I was walking home from Summer's to help Tat begin work on the repair of his foundation. As I strolled innocently along I suddenly felt someone walking right behind me.

"Keep walking," he said.

"Who are you?" I asked, not feeling the least bit threatened by whoever he actually was.

"If you'll turn at the next break in the path, I'll tell you."

I wasn't too curious, seeing how I could see no real reason why I needed to know him. But I knew Tat would be fine working on the foundation without me for a few minutes so I turned and walked into the forested brush just off of Waffer Lane. After we had taken about twenty steps into the green I asked, "So do I get to know who you are now?"

"A bit more," he motioned.

Two minutes later we stopped behind a large cluster of thick trees. A bird up above yelled at us for a couple of seconds and then flew off. I took a quick second to size up this man I had so willingly allowed to lead me off. He was probably about my age. He was a little over 5'10" with a fat nose and eyes that were uneven in both placement and color. His top lip rolled up when he spoke, giving me a clear glimpse of the gum between his two front teeth and plump nose. He was pale and uneasy.

"This sure is a pretty spot," I said. "Thanks for bringing me here."

My comment confused him.

"You're Andy, right?" He pointed at me as if I might not have been sure whether he meant me or the tree I was standing next to.

"I am. And you are?"

"I'm Larry Cutler."

I sort of couldn't get my eyes or mouth to move. I could actually feel my brain trying to make sense of what I was hearing.

"I read all about what's been going on and I felt I needed to talk to you," he went on. "The papers say you really did a number figuring this all out. Thanks." He meekly bowed.

"I can't believe it," I said in amazement. "So you really aren't dead."

"Nope," Larry smiled. "I could have been. Pitt threatened to kill us before we flew off. We were so scared. So when I lost control of the plane right after takeoff and we splashed down in Knock Pond we didn't know what to do. We landed rather gracefully and were able to swim to the shore unhurt. But while we were walking back into town it occurred to Tillie and I that this might be our one chance. We set off towards the South and never looked back."

"Why did Pitt threaten you?" I asked.

"Because of my dad's paint formula," Larry said proudly. "My father invented it. Best paint in the world. Stands up under almost any condition. Problem was that too many of the fumes made people sleepy. My dad was scared that folks would be falling off ladders while painting their houses. But Pitt didn't care," Larry continued. He was angry. "He just saw the dollar signs. The doctors said my father had a heart attack, but I know it was Pitt. The funny thing is that after my dad passed away, Pitt discovered that he couldn't find the formula."

It wasn't that funny, but I didn't want to point that out.

"Pitt came after me," Larry went on. "He thought that maybe I had the formula. When I realized how desperate he was for it, I also realized that he might have had something to do with my dad's death. I confronted Pitt and he told me that the day I said anything like that in public would be my last day on earth."

"Wow."

"Both Tillie and I had always wanted to get away from here and see the world anyway," Larry continued. "We figured our fallen plane was a sign. A chance to begin our lives somewhere else."

"So where did you end up?" I asked.

"Odessa, Texas."

They were really seeing the world.

"Why'd you come here now?"

"I needed to fill you in before you found us. The newspapers made it clear that you don't give up until you've solved the whole case. Tillie and I have been worrying all week. We don't want to be found. We have a good life and it would only ruin things if we had to appear again."

"What about your family here?" I asked. "Shouldn't you tell them?"

"Listen, Andy," Larry whispered. "To be quite honest with you, my family and I didn't really have the best relationship before I died. But I'm not all coldhearted. That's why I brought you this note to give to my mother. I also wrote down what I know of Pitt and his doings. I don't care if people know we're alive; I just care about those same people figuring out where we are."

"How should I say I got the letters?"

"I don't know," Larry complained. "You're the detective."

"Well, actually . . ."

"Will you do this for us, Andy?" he asked. "Tell them you think we're in Alaska, or Russia. Heck, I don't care. Just don't find us."

"I'll pass out the letters and keep my mouth shut." It was the best I could promise.

"Bless you, Andy."

I took a moment to feel blessed and then I watched as Larry slipped off into the trees and back into hiding. I walked back to the trail and then turned and headed to Summer's.

I couldn't wait to tell her about the new friend I had just made.

CHAPTER THIRTY-FIVE

RINGY DINGY

I'm embarrassed to say it, but I attained legendary status by handing over those letters. They solved the mystery of what had happened to Larry and Tillie, as well as explaining just why Pitt had been so desperate to get that formula.

I was feeling so impressed with myself that I even explained to everyone that the reason Mishap had been so tired lately was most likely due to the paint on the plane that had been soaking at the bottom of the water system for so long. The same plane that had been exposed during storms to reflect the moonlight and cast images upon Knock Pond. It could have been the town's obsession with the curse, or maybe it was just fate playing tricks on us, but I know firsthand that those images had looked remarkably like Harriet Hap.

Summer was the only one who saw me for what I really was. In fact, I was considering being offended by how quickly she believed me when I confessed that I had not, and could not, have solved these mysteries myself.

"It'll be our little secret," she teased.

"It'll be your little secret if you want," I argued. "But I'm going to prove to the world that I'm not capable of actually figuring things out."

"It seems like that would be an easy case to make," Summer said casually.

She was mistaken. The whole town thought I could do no wrong. I gave up even trying to temper their appreciation and compliments. I was a detective by default, but no one wanted to accept that. I thought there was no way that I could impress people any further until the phone call.

I was down in the Harding house basement watching a movie with Summer, and Ariel and Sarah, and Gordon and Lauren, and Bert and a very pregnant Annie, when Phyllis came into the room and informed me I had a phone call. Since I was in the presence of Summer I couldn't imagine there being anyone I wanted to talk to on the other side. But I climbed upstairs and picked up the receiver that was lying on the counter.

"Hello?"

"Hello," a raspy voice said back. "Is this Andy Phillips?"

"It is," I answered, assuming it was simply another TV or radio show wanting an interview from me.

"You don't know me," the voice went on, "but I used to live there in Thunder City. My name is Harriet Hap."

I couldn't believe it. "Mrs. Hap? I know you."

"I thought you might," she whispered. "The papers say you're a pretty shrewd detective."

I considered telling her that the reason I knew her was not because I had cleverly discovered it, but because I currently lived in a town that was nicknamed after her. Plus, I had been the one to find her husband dead. I had also dived into what was then thought to be her face stretched out across Knock

Pond. Not to mention that there wasn't a day that went by that some conversation in this town didn't revolve around her.

I let her talk.

"I read about you finding Larry and Tillie," she said. "I guess I'm just a little frightened about you finding me. Thunder City is a memory I'd like never to think about again. I don't know what kind of deal you made with Larry Cutler, but I'm willing to pay to have you keep silent."

I didn't have the heart to tell her that if she hadn't called me her presence would have never been discovered—at least not by me that is.

"Mrs. Hap, I don't want your money," I said, supressing the thought of how much I would like a new car. "I just think that it might be a good idea for you to call the authorities and let them know where you are, and that you're alive. I've heard rumors that they are considering charging Pitt Frank with your murder."

"Pitt didn't kill me," she snapped.

"I know that," I said. "But they think he killed your husband—"

"Ex-husband," she interrupted.

"Ex-husband." I appeased her. "They're also opening up Willard Cutler's case again to see if there was any foul play there. The last thing Pitt needs is to be charged for your murder seeing how you're not dead and all."

There was a long pause.

"It would serve Pitt right to be charged with my murder," she finally said. "He was a big part of all that was wrong between Reinhold and me. He was greedy and driven. Reinhold took all his frustration he had for Pitt out on our marriage."

"I'm sorry," I said. "But I still think it might be best if you let the authorities know you're alive."

"I don't have to," she snapped.

"Mrs. Hap," I tried to sound as if I were scolding her.

There was a tremendous sigh and then she said, "I suppose if I don't then you'll just find out where I am anyhow."

I looked at the caller ID and read her her own phone number.

"You're good," she whispered in awe.

"Will you call them?" I asked.

"Will you keep my phone number and residence a secret?"

"I will; I promise."

"Thank you, Mr. Phillips," she said cordially.

"Thank you, Mrs. Hap."

I hung up and walked back downstairs. The movie had ended in my absence and everyone was talking about what a dumb show it was and how any one of them could have made a much better one. I sat back down next to Summer.

"Who was on the phone?" she asked.

"Harriet Hap," I said.

Everyone turned to look at me.

"Mrs. Hap!" Gordon exclaimed.

I took a few moments to go over the finer points of detective work and how I never rested until I cleaned up the case completely. They then took a couple of seconds to compliment and congratulate me on a job well done. Of course by "they" I mean everyone except Summer. She simply smiled, willing to wait patiently for the time when the two of us would be alone and I could tell her the true story. The story about everything having fallen into my lap again.

I was going to say a few more things about myself when Annie rudely interrupted the conversation by telling us her water had broken. We all rushed around as Bert helped her up the stairs and into the car. Summer went with the two of them to the hospital leaving me alone with everyone else.

The next call I received that day was from Bert. He was phoning to see if he had left his favorite ball cap there, and to inform us that thirty minutes ago their son Richard Lawson was born.

We were all deliriously happy for him.

CHAPTER THIRTY-SIX

THE FEELING OF FULFILLMENT

In 2001 a man by the name of Andy Phillips came to Thunder City to teach school and experience the West. As an easterner he had thought the opportunity would make him more understanding and well-rounded. As a Mormon he had hoped that the chance to live with a large number of Saints would be calming and fulfilling. Both of his desires were realized, although the path to those realizations was one that he would never have anticipated.

I looked out over those gathered as I sat next to Summer and smiled. Summer wore a feather in her hair like all the other women in attendance. I donned a construction-paper pilgrim hat so as to match the rest of the men. Bishop Hearth was at the head of the table smiling and going on about how thankful he was for everything. His comments were appropriate, seeing how it was our ward Thanksgiving dinner celebration. Long banquet tables had been set up next to each other in one continuous line. Though that line was bent and squared where necessary, we were all straight in the condition of our souls.

We were all very grateful.

"If you'll humor me I'd like to do something a little different this year," Bishop Hearth said while standing before us. "It seems that in the past I saw so many of you simply as residents of Thunder City and of our ward. I have to say that this last six months our congregation has grown in leaps and bounds." He turned to Phyllis who was standing in the doorway near the church kitchen. "Can the turkeys cook a few minutes longer?" he asked her.

She nodded an affirmative.

"What I would like is to go around the table and for all of us to briefly share what we're thankful for."

There was some mild whispering and nodding as we digested what was being asked of us on an empty stomach.

"Let me begin," Bishop Hearth said, his composure beginning to wane. "I am grateful for my family. For my wife," he smiled at Maggie, "and for my new job."

Bishop Hearth was Mishap's newest barber. A few months back Whip's hair allergies became so severe that all a person had to do was ask for a haircut and he would start sneezing on the spot. When he announced his retirement, Burton Hearth stepped forward and admitted that he had always wanted to cut hair. It wasn't easy—or more appropriately put—it was pretty messy, but Whip taught Burton all he knew. He then handed him the keys to the store and left Mishap to see the country in an RV. Bishop Hearth had turned out to be one skilled hairdresser. He also used his occupation to ease his burden as bishop. It wasn't unusual for him to offer you a new calling or give you an interview while he was trimming you up. In fact I had received my calling as ward mission leader while getting a shave. Bishop Hearth's new job had done wonders to the look of our town and to the Hearth marriage. His being able to stay in town for work was a great family perk.

Georgia Loft was the next person to say what she was grateful for. "I'm thankful for honesty and kindness," she said as her dented shoulders shuttered.

I was tempted to inform her that those were cop-out things to be thankful for because everyone wanted honesty and kindness. But the way Sister Loft said what she said spoke more than the actual words she had used.

Everyone knew that Georgia was speaking of Pitt and the mess that he had made by being dishonest and unkind to the very people he had once claimed to care for. Because of what had happened, the Council of Seven was no more. Its end had come about by the conviction of Pitt. Thanks to Larry Cutler's letter and renewed interest in Willard Cutler's death, Pitt was charged and convicted of sins greater than any man on earth could ever absolve. Authorities had now charged him with the death of Reinhold. Pitt was lucky that Harriet Hap had kept her part of the deal and had let authorities know she was actually alive. I felt pretty certain that Pitt would have been held accountable for her supposed death as well if she had not come forward.

Pitt's wife left town to live with her parents in Salt Lake and his brother Respect returned to Mishap and took over the gravel business. Respect was a tiny man with a quick wit and a warm smile. It was as if the Frank family gene pool liked to keep the positive and negative completely separated. Respect was called to be the ward activities director and was working hard to convince people that the Frank name was not all bad. Due to Pitt's incarceration, the Council of Seven had dipped down to a much less impressive Council of Five. So they decided to go out on a low note and disband without fanfare or festivity.

Mishap was on its own in the decision making department.

As the ward continued to admit publicly what they were thankful for we all grew more and more moved. Bryan Find was thankful for patience. Vinton Moore? He was grateful for time and the ability to change. The Tart boys were happy for food and cars. Debby Simmons couldn't seem to say enough about music and the golden vocal chords that she had been given. If I had been directly after her I would have been thankful for the fact that she hadn't given us a demonstration of her "golden vocal cords." But Gordon came after Debby.

I could tell that Gordon was worried about being able to get anything out. Emotionally he was wavering. The smell of the food and the objects of gratitude that had already been mentioned made the air as fulfilling as a week's worth of visions and miracles.

"I'm thankful for . . . " Gordon couldn't do it. He picked up his napkin and pretended that he had a cold.

Lauren and Gordon were still dating. They started strong, and a little weird, and then things cooled down a bit after Lauren returned to Charlotte to sort out her feelings for Gordon. Despite the fact that Lauren was fine with his religion, her family was still giving them fits. Worried he was losing her, Gordon drove all the way to North Carolina and surprised her by waking her up at three in the morning to announce that he had just arrived and couldn't live without her. Lauren was not only flattered, but she was reminded that Gordon was handsome in a Gonzala Heratio sort of way. She had come out to visit him once since then and he had been back twice. According to the last conversation I had with Gordon, the plan was for Lauren to fly out here in a couple of weeks to spend Christmas in Mishap. If all went well there was the possibility that the two of them could be married by Easter.

If the union of Gordon and Lauren did come to pass, it wouldn't be the first marriage since the curse had been lifted. Because, in exactly four days, Sarah Harding was set to marry Ariel Backer. The wedding was to take place in the Provo Temple with the blessing of not only Tat and Phyllis, but of the whole town. It would be the first marriage since the curse had been officially proven phony.

Right after Ariel and Sarah made the announcement of their engagement, Tat had secretly slipped me a twenty-dollar bill. He thanked me for showing Sarah that extra little attention I had once promised I would. When I reminded Tat that I had only taught Sarah for a few days before our marriage class had fallen apart all those months ago, he simply said, "Those must have been a couple of powerful days."

Those days had nothing over on the ones I was now experiencing. It seemed that every morning when I woke up my body and soul were that much more attached to the small world around me. I loved Mishap. I loved the goofy chapel and the wide, funny-named streets. I had a testimony of the beauty of the deep red cliffs, and I had publicly declared my devotion to the Wayne River and the beauty it brought in. Of course, as wonderful as those things were, they would have been nothing without the knowledge that they came with some of the best people I had ever known.

I watched Lilith Stern thank the heavens for her husband, Gary, and for a Creator that saw fit to make us imperfect enough to need a little foundation and blush. Gary followed his wife by giving thanks for indoor plumbing and a robust economy. I was grateful for the Sterns and their less-than-sappy gratitude. The things they were thankful for were light enough to help me get my own emotions in check.

Four folks down from the Sterns, Nick Goodfellow stood and admitted that he was thankful for truth and for the fact that God didn't work in curses and rumors. He held up his water glass and toasted the blessing of our now nontainted drinking water.

Everyone toasted back.

Just last week the improvements and reconstruction of Knock Pond had been completed. I had been there only yesterday to witness the water level rising very slowly. With the work the state had done, the new boundaries of the pond would increase our body of water by almost a third. Everyone was impatiently waiting to see the finished product.

Nick was also thankful for Shelly Simmons, who was willing to date him now that he had started parting his hair on the opposite side, and that there was no longer a curse hovering over us.

Wilson Phelps surprised us all by bringing up Reinhold Hap and blessing the life that our town had done wrong. We were all quiet as the words settled. Wilson went on to say that he now understood how one life could affect generations and that he hoped his own might amount to something worth passing on.

When Reinhold had passed away we had all been so caught up in what was going on elsewhere that no one had stopped to realize that it might be nice to give him a funeral. A month after the earthquake and while everything was beginning to fall into place, Sister Peggy Tart pointed out what we had forgotten. The entire town then gathered at the Thunder City park and held a memorial for Reinhold. Randall Crammer had even constructed a statue in memory of the late Mr. Hap. The statue was in the form of the right half of a tall tree. Randall explained that he had gotten the inspiration from me cutting up his and Chad's chicken. The half of tree that you saw clearly showed what we were, while the half that wasn't there gave indication of what we could be. The partial tree stood proudly next to the big frog statue in the center of the city.

It was amazing to think of just how many days had passed since I stood there in horror with Randall, Chad, and that poor chicken. Now Randall was creating statues and Chad had finally gotten the stereo he had been working so hard to earn. Of course he actually ended up getting much more than just a radio. Yep, Chad was now the proud owner of my old car. I had tried to get it working about three months ago but soon discovered that there was more than just a weak battery keeping it from rolling. Chad heard about my dilemma and about the fact that the only thing that worked on the vehicle was the stereo. He gave me thirty dollars, bought a new car battery, and now spent most of his free time sitting out in front of Gordon's store listening to music in his stalled stereo.

A couple of families offered group gratitude, as we moved down the tables. Then Brother Farrelly, the ward's second counselor thanked heaven for the unknown angel who had been inspired enough to saw down our pews. It was no mystery as to why our ward was finally becoming the kind of gathering that our Father in Heaven had hoped it would be, he said. It was as if the veil had been lifted and we could all now see with our spiritual eyes. The effect of the shortened pews had been so powerful that the bishopric had taken it a step further by removing one of the rows and repositioning the pews, thus giving the whole ward more leg room. Sure there was some confusion the morning we collectively discovered that not only had the pews been thinned out, they had also not been bolted back down. But, after everyone got back in place and the seats were bolted down, we all reveled in the comfort and serenity our revamped chapel provided.

I had been so deep in thought concerning the state of our flock that I almost missed Tat as he told us all what he was grateful for.

"For Phil, of course." He sniffed. "And my girls." He teared up. "And my grandson and my soon-to-be son-in-law, Ariel." He cried. "I have always hated Thanksgiving ever since my father passed away. Turkey and the weather make the memories of my dad almost too heavy to bear. But this year feels different." Tat dried his eyes. Then as if he had no idea how close I was to losing my facade, he thanked his brother back in Charlotte for sending me out to Mishap. He then looked at me and smiled.

He was so cruel.

After Tat came Summer. I started looking for things I could do in my seat that would distract me from what she was saying and thus prevent me from turning into a blubbering idiot. I refolded my napkin as she said kind things about her parents. I scooted my chair up a couple of inches and then back a few trying to find the perfect position while she confessed how grateful she was for the ward. I then fiddled with the salt shaker as she began to cry and talk about how happy she was that a guy from back east had been brave enough to try a little Utah. She sat down and kissed me.

It was my turn. I looked over everyone there and sighed. I saw faces of people that I now knew as more than just neighbors. I saw in each member the things we had been through, the places they lived, the problems they had, and the touch of the divine imprinted in their faces.

Summer nudged me.

I stood and cleared my throat. "I don't know what to say," I said. "I can't thank you all enough for what you've done for me." My throat warbled. "If I even start to think about life without Tat and . . . " I was just about to break down and blubber to them all about how much I liked each and every one of them when smoke began to billow out of the kitchen. Phyllis and a couple of other women ran to investigate.

The turkey was ruined and I couldn't have been happier. The distraction saved me from having to sob more. By the time the smoke cleared we had all forgotten that I had been stopped midsentence. We passed around the side dishes and talked and ate as if we were all in the waiting room of heaven. It would have felt quite natural for a glowing angel to pop in and inform us that it was our turn to enter.

Wanting to step away for a moment, I told Summer I needed to use the restroom and slipped out into the hall. With the doors leading into the festivity closed it was quiet and peaceful. I walked down past the bishop's office and turned the corner to see Maggie coming my way. We stopped a couple of feet away from each other.

"Happy Thanksgiving, Andy." She smiled.

"Same to you."

"Thanks for everything you've done."

I wondered if she was referring to the few times I had watched her children so that she and her husband could go out.

"I didn't do anything," I said, hoping she would clarify just what it was that she was thanking me for. She didn't. She just patted me on the arm and walked down the hall humming.

I was about seven steps away from the bathroom when I spotted Lauren coming in through the side door. She was wearing a small jacket and a huge smile.

"What are you doing here?" I asked. I was surprised and happy to see her.

"I can't stay away," she grinned. "I flew in to Salt Lake this morning. I'm hoping to surprise Gordon."

"I think you'll have no problem doing that."

Then for the second time in five minutes a ghost of a girlfriend past thanked me for something unspecific and vague. "Thanks, Andy," Lauren said, patting the opposite arm that Maggie had.

"I didn't do anything," I humbly insisted.

"You did."

After a pause she asked, "Where's Gordon?"

I pointed in the right direction and she left me. I watched her walk around the corner and soon heard Gordon screech with joy as they reunited. I walked into the bathroom and stared at myself in the mirror. I don't know if it was the lighting or my mood but for some reason my eyes looked bluer than they had eight months ago. I ran my fingers through my hair and washed my hands even though they weren't dirty. Steam rose from the warm water and fogged up the bottom two inches of the mirror. I could feel the warmth in my eyes and wondered if this was what revelation felt like.

I looked back into the mirror and saw a giant turkey standing next to me. I jumped at least three feet.

"You've got some real spring in those knees," I heard Tat say from within the costume.

"What are you doing?"

"Phil found this costume at a shop in Salt Lake. She figured it would really add to the festivities."

"It adds," I said.

"I just came in here to adjust my neck," Tat said as he jiggled the large gobbler that hung from his foam head. "Actually, Andy, I'm glad to get you alone. I'm afraid I've done something bad."

"Really?"

"I read one of your letters," he confessed as he brushed his feathers.

"Tat, that's nothing new."

"I wrote a reply back to the sender."

"You answered my mail?"

"I used a dictionary to make you sound smart. I think you would have been pleased with your word choices."

I think he wanted me to thank him.

"Would it be all right for you to tell me who the letter was from?"

Tat thought for a moment as he tugged at the orange leggings that he had on. "Okay, here's the deal. Apparently that old school you used to work at back east is finished being rebuilt and they want you back. I simply let them know that you weren't interested and that you were actually quite philanthropistic that they would even ask."

I shook my head in amazement. "When you said you used a dictionary did you actually read what the words meant or did you just pick ones that looked impressive?"

"Presentation is everything, Andy." He tested his wings and then gobbled.

I watched the steam fill the mirror like a veil, shadowing me from myself. I still wasn't completely sure about what the future held and I told Tat so.

"Don't make it so complicated that you can't figure it out," he advised. "I remember when I was fourteen, right after I won first prize for woodworking at the Scout jamboree. I was just about as full of myself as I could be. I saw all sorts of possibilities for my talents and gifts. Well, my father in his wisdom pulled me aside and showed me this."

Tat pulled out an extremely worn piece of paper that looked like it had been a bookmark at some point in its existence.

"Wow," I said flatly.

"I carry it with me wherever I go," Tat said reflectively. "My father got it from the drugstore years ago. They were giving them out to anyone they did business with. It's got a poem about not quitting written on it."

I watched the steam, wondering if I needed to respond.

"My dad saw me getting confused by the turns and peaks of life," Tat said, putting a wing on my shoulder. "So he pointed out that this bookmark would probably influence more lives for good than I ever would. He wasn't being mean, or putting me down, he was simply reminding me not to take myself so seriously."

Tat handed me the bookmark and smiled as wide as his costume would allow.

"I can't take this," I protested.

"I think it would help me if you did."

"Thanks, Tat," I said, wondering if it were the steam or my emotions that were choking me up.

Phyllis stuck her head in the bathroom and informed her husband that he was on. He left me alone to look in the mirror and evaluate. I read the poem on the bookmark and then stuck it in my pocket. My life felt right but I still wouldn't have minded if heaven had taken a moment to tell me that I was finally on track.

As I stepped out of the bathroom Summer was there looking for me.

"What are you doing?" I asked her.

"I'm not sure," she said smiling. "I think I was beginning to miss you."

"That's odd, don't you think?"

"Extremely," she agreed. "People can grow attached to the strangest things."

"That's true. My mother used to sleep with her toothbrush." I had a tremendous ability to ruin the mood. "When she was a kid," I clarified, as if that made it any better.

We both stood there looking at each other. It was no secret that Summer and I were in love. The town always included us whenever it listed off those that were in line to marry someday. Sure, we had not actually made it official, but just as I had once felt that Lauren wasn't my future, I now knew that Summer was.

"What are you thinking about, Andy?" she asked as I stared at her.

"We're old enough to be married," I said dreamily.

"That's true," she agreed.

"And I've been told that matrimony is important."

"You can't believe everything you hear, but that seems a safe assumption."

"It might be crazy," I smiled, "but would you marry me?"

"Sure," she said casually.

"I'm not joking," I informed her.

"Neither am I."

"I'm talking about the kind of marriage where people live together and have kids and occasional fights and maybe get matching robes."

"That's the kind of marriage I'm envisioning."

"Even the robes?"

"Andy, do you want me to marry you?"

"More than anything."

It was no different than jumping from a tree or diving into Knock Pond. The reaction just pushed up into me until I had hold of Summer and was kissing her like I envisioned Adam first kissing Eve. I felt her dark hair in my fingers and through my closed eyes I saw everything I loved about her become clearer and clearer. My head was suddenly filled with trumpets and harps, and I pulled her even closer. Eventually we both remembered that this was a telestial state we were presently living in and that we needed to come back down and visit.

Bert and Annie Lawson came in through the front doors with their son Richard. They walked up to Summer and me.

"Sorry we're late," Annie apologized. "Bert had to work until eight."

"Did we miss anything?" Bert asked.

Summer and I simply smiled.

As soon as the Lawsons had walked off I took Summer by the hand and led her to the broom closet. We opened the false wall and stepped into the system of tunnels I had been introduced to when Pitt was still around.

We spent the rest of the night getting ourselves properly lost.